THE HAND OF DEATH

WEBB HOLT STOOD with his feet spread, his right side toward Tap Henry. His gun butt was on his right hip, the butt end to the fore and canted a mite.

"Look," he said, "we don't need to—" He grabbed iron and Tap shot him twice through the chest.

"Lucky you warned me about that left hand," Tap said. "I might have made a mistake."

We rounded up the cattle and drove them home, and nobody said anything, at any time.

Bantam Books by Louis L'Amour

KILLOE

A NOVEL

Louis L'Amour

BANTAM BOOKS
NEW YORK

2021 Bantam Books Mass Market Edition

Copyright © 1967 by Louis D. & Katherine E. L'Amour 1983 Trust

Excerpt from *Law of the Desert Born, A Graphic Novel*
by Louis L'Amour, script by Beau L'Amour and Katherine Nolan,
text copyright © 2013 by Beau L'Amour and illustrations
copyright © 2013 by Louis L'Amour Enterprises, Inc.

Published in the United States by Bantam Books,
an imprint of Random House, a division of
Penguin Random House LLC, New York.

Bantam Books and the House colophon are registered trademarks of
Penguin Random House LLC.

Originally published in paperback in the United States by
Bantam Books, an imprint of Random House, a division of
Penguin Random House LLC, in 1962, 1971, 1996, and 2003.

ISBN 978-0-553-25742-7
Ebook ISBN 978-0-553-89931-3

Cover art: Gregory Manchess

Printed in the United States of America

randomhousebooks.com

76 78 80 82 83 81 79 77 75

Bantam Books mass market edition: July 2021

To Bill Tilghman: Frontier Marshal
who showed me how it was done with a six-gun

————————————————

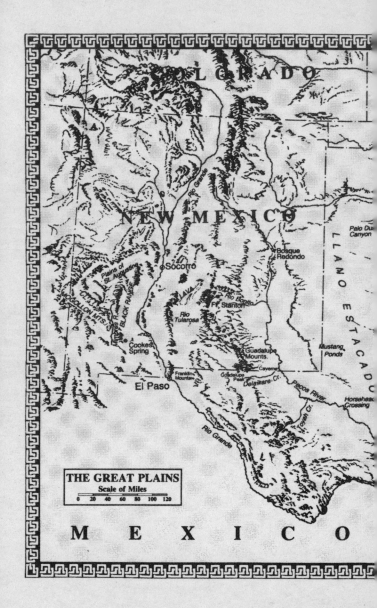

COLORADO

NEW MEXICO

Palo Duro Canyon

LLANO ESTACADO

Bosque Redondo

Plains of St. Augustine

Socorro

Rio Bonito

Ft. Stanton

Rio Tularosa

MOGOLLON MTS.

Tutas R.

BLACK RANGE

Cookes Spring

Mustang Ponds

Guadalupe Mounts.

Cayeme

Franklin Mountains

Guadalupe Peak

Delaware Cr.

Pecos River

El Paso

Horsehead Crossing

Rio Grande

Toyah Cr.

THE GREAT PLAINS
Scale of Miles
0   20   40   60   80   100   120

MEXICO

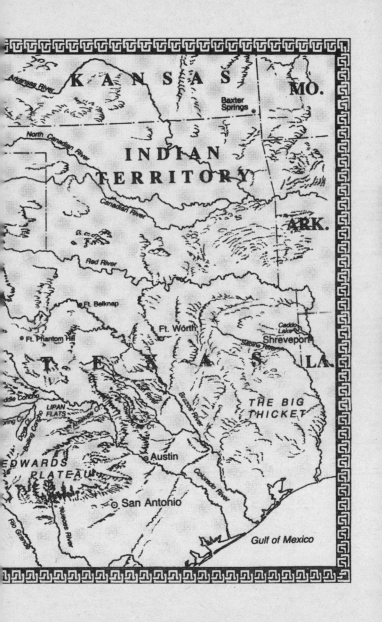

KILLOE

CHAPTER 1

PA CAME DOWN to the breaks along the Cowhouse where I was rousting out some steers that had taken to the brush because of the heel-flies.

"Come up to the house, boy. Tap has come home and he is talking of the western lands."

So I gathered my rope to a coil and slung it on the pommel of my saddle, and stepping up to the leather, I followed Pa up through the trees and out on the open grass.

Folks were standing in the breezeway of our Texas house, and others were grouped around in bunches, listening to Tap Henry or talking among themselves.

It was not a new thing, for there had been argument and discussion going on for weeks. We all knew that something must be done, and westward the land was empty.

Tap Henry was a tall man of twenty-seven or -eight and we had been boys together, although he was a good six to seven years older than me. A hard, reckless man with a taste for wild country and wilder living, he was a top hand in any man's outfit, and a good man with a gun.

You couldn't miss Tap Henry. He was well over six feet tall and weighed a compact one hundred and ninety. He wore a freshly laundered blue shield-style shirt with a row of buttons down each side, shotgun chaps, and Spanish boots with big California spurs.

He still packed that pearl-handled six-shooter he had taken off a man he had killed, and he was handsome as ever in that hard, flashy way of his. He was our friend and, in a sense, he was my brother.

Our eyes met across the heads of the others as I rode up, and his were cold and measuring. It was a look I had seen in his eyes before, but never directed at me. It was the way he looked when he saw a possible antagonist. Recognition came suddenly to his eyes.

"Danny! Dan, boy!" He strode through the crowd that had gathered to hear his talk of the lands to the west, and thrust out a hand. "Well, I'll be forever damned! You've grown up!"

Stepping down from the saddle, I met his grip with one of my own, remembering how Tap prided himself on his strength. For a moment I matched him, grip for grip, then let him have the better of it, for he was a proud man and I liked him, and I had nothing to prove.

It surprised me that we stood eye to eye, for he had always seemed very tall, and I believe it surprised him, too.

Almost involuntarily, his eyes dropped to my belt, but I was wearing no gun. My rifle was in my saddle-boot and my knife was in its sheath.

"We're going west, Danny!" His hand on my shoulder, we walked back to where Pa now stood with Aaron Stark and Tim Foley. "I've scouted the land, and there is grass enough, and more!"

Pa glanced curiously from one to the other of us, and from the shadow of the breezeway Zebony

Lambert watched us, a strange light in his green eyes. Zeb's long brown hair lay about his shoulders, as carefully combed as a woman's, his eyes level and hard under the flat brim of his Spanish hat.

Zebony Lambert was my friend, but I do not think he had many friends, for he was a solitary, self-keeping sort of man little given to talk. Of medium height, his extraordinarily broad shoulders made him seem shorter, and they were well set off by the short Spanish jacket he wore, and the buckskin, bell-bottomed breeches.

Lambert and Tap had never met until now, and it worried me a little, for both were strong men, and Tap was inclined toward arrogance.

"Is it true, then?" I asked Pa. "Is it decided?"

"Aye ... we're going west, Dan."

Tim Foley was our neighbor who ran a few cows of his own, but occasionally worked for us. A square-built man with a square, honest face. "And high time," he said, "for there is little grass and we have those about us who like us not at all."

"How far is it, then?"

"Six hundred miles or less. Right across Texas and into New Mexico. If we do not go on, it will be less."

Pa looked at me. More and more he was paying mind to my judgment, and listening to what I had to say. He was still the boss ... I knew that and he knew it, but he had respect for my judgment, which had grown since he had been leaving the cattle business to me.

"How many head, Dan? What can we muster?" Pa put the question and I caught a surprised look from Tap, for he remembered me as a boy, and a boy only.

"Fifteen hundred at least, and I'd say a bit more than that. Tim will have a good three hundred head under his own brand, and Aaron nearly as many. When all are rounded up and the breaks swept clean, I would say close to three thousand head."

"It is a big herd, and we will be short of men," Pa commented thoughtfully.

"There will be three wagons, and the horse herd," I added.

"Wagons?" Tap objected. "I hadn't planned on wagons."

"We have our families," Tim said, "and there are tools we must take."

There began a discussion of what to take, of trail problems and men, and I leaned against the corral rail, listening without paying much attention. In every such venture there is always more talk than is necessary, with everybody having his say, but I knew that when all was said, much of it would be left to me, and I would do as seemed best to me.

There is no point in such endless discussion, except that men become familiar with their problems. Long ago, when the first discussion of such a move began, I had also begun thinking of it, and had made some plans I thought necessary. Lambert, a thoughtful man, had contributed a few pointed and common-sense suggestions.

We could muster barely a dozen men, far too few for the task that lay ahead. Once the herd was trail-broke, four to five men might keep it moving without much trouble, but until then it would be a fight. Some of these old mossyhorns had grown up there on the Cowhouse and they had no wish to leave home.

There would be the usual human problems, too, even though the people who would be accompanying our move would all be known to us. And once away from the settlements, there would be Comanches.

It was a risk, a big risk. We were chancing everything.

We might have fought it out where we were, but Pa was no hand for a fight, although he had courage enough for two men, and had seen his share of fighting in the Mexican War and with Indians. He had grown up in the Five Counties and knew what feuding meant. It was Tap who had suggested going west, and Pa fell in with it.

But there was risk connected with everything, and we were hard men bred to a hard life in a hard land, and the lives that we lived were lonely, yet rich with the voice of our singing, and with tales told of an evening by the campfire.

What pleasures we had were created by ourselves or born of the land, our clothing was made by our own hands, our houses and corrals, also. Those who rode beside us knew the measure of our strength as we knew theirs, and each knew the courage of the other.

In that country a man saddled his own broncs and fought his own battles, and the measure of his manhood was that he did what needed to be done, and did it well, and without shirking.

Me? I, Dan Killoe, was born in a claim cabin on Cowhouse Creek with the roar of buffalo guns filling the room as Pa and my Uncle Fred beat off an Indian attack. I let out my first yell in a room filled with gunsmoke, and when Ma died I was nursed by a Mexican woman whose father died fighting with the Texans at the Alamo.

When I was six, Pa met Tap's Ma on a trip to Fort Worth, and married her, bringing her west to live with us, and they brought Tap along.

She was a pretty woman, as I recall, and good enough to us boys, but she wasn't cut out for frontier life, and finally she cut and run with some no-account drifter, leaving Tap to live with us.

Tap always pulled his weight, and more. He took to cow country like he was born to it, and we got along. He was thirteen and doing a man's work and proud of it, for the difference between a man and a boy is the willingness to do a man's work and take a man's responsibility.

Being older than me, he was always the leader, no matter what we were doing, and a few times when we had a chance to attend school, he took up for me when I might have taken a beating from bigger boys.

When Tap pulled out the first time he was seventeen and I was a bit more than ten. He was gone most of a year, working for some outfit over in the Big Thicket.

The next time I saw him he was wearing a pistol, and we heard rumors he had killed a man over near Caddo Lake.

When he was at home he worked like all get-out, but he soon had the name of being a good man to let alone. Pa said nothing much to him, only dropping a comment now and then, and Tap always listened, or seemed to. But he was gone most of the time after that, and each time he came back he was bigger, tougher, and more sure of himself.

It had been three years since we had last seen Tap,

but now he was back, and at the right time, too. Trouble was building along the Cowhouse and neighbors were crowding in, and it was time we moved west and laid claim to land.

We would be leaving mighty little on the Cowhouse. When Pa moved into the country a body couldn't live there at all without neighbors and they bunched up for protection. Some died and some were killed, some drifted and some sold out, but the country changed and the people, and now it was building into a fight for range.

Some of the newcomers had no cattle, and from time to time they would kill a beef of ours. Pa was no one to keep a man's youngsters from food, so he allowed it. The trouble was, they turned from killing a beef for food to driving them off and selling them, and trouble was cropping up.

A couple of times I'd caught men with our brand on some steers they were driving, and I drove them back, but twice shots had been fired at me.

The old crop that worked hard and fought hard for their homes were gone. This new lot seemed to figure they could live off what we had worked for, and it was developing into trouble. What we wanted was land that belonged to us—land with boundaries and lines drawn plain and clear; but due to the way everybody had started out on the Cowhouse, that wasn't true here.

There was talk of moving west, and then Tap rode in, fresh from that country.

Pa was a farmer at heart, more interested in crops than cattle, and of late I'd taken to running the cattle business.

"It is a bad trip, I'll not lie about that," Tap was saying. "But the time of year is right, and if we start soon there will be grass and water."

"And when we get there?" Foley asked.

"The best grass you ever saw, and water, too. We can stop on the Pecos in New Mexico, or we can go on to Colorado."

"What would you suggest?" Foley was a shrewd man, and he was keeping a close watch on Tap as he questioned him.

"The Pecos country. Near Bosque Redondo."

Karen Foley came to stand beside me, her eyes watching Tap. "Isn't he exciting?" she said. "I'm glad he will be with us."

For the first time I felt a twinge of jealousy, but it was a small twinge, for I liked and admired Tap Henry myself, and I knew what she meant.

Tap was different. He had come riding back into our lives wearing better clothes than we could afford, riding a fine chestnut gelding with a beautifully hand-tooled saddle, the first one I had ever seen. Moreover, he carried himself with a kind of style.

He had a hard, sure way about him and he walked and moved with an assurance we did not have. You felt there was no uncertainty about Tap Henry, that he knew what he wanted and knew how to get it. Only faintly, and with a twinge of guilt, did I think that perhaps he cared too little for the feelings or interests of others. Nevertheless, I could think of no better man on a trip of the kind we were planning.

Karen was another thing, for Karen and I had been walking out together, talking a little, and a couple of times we had taken rides together. We had no understanding or anything like it, but she was the prettiest girl anywhere around, and for a girl out on the Texas plains she got herself up mighty well.

She was the oldest of Tim Foley's three children. The other two were boys, fourteen and ten.

It was plain she was taken by Tap Henry, and one thing I knew about Tap was that he was no man to take lightly where women were concerned. He had a way with them, and they took to him.

Pa turned around. "Come over here, Dan. We want your advice."

Tap laughed as I walked up, and clapped a hand on my shoulder in that way he had. "What's the matter, Killoe? You taking advice from kids now?"

"Dan knows more about cattle than anybody I ever knew," Pa said quietly, "and this won't be his first trail drive."

"You?" Tap was surprised. "A trail drive?"

"Uh-huh. I took a herd through Baxter Springs last year. Took them through to Illinois and sold them."

"Baxter Springs?" Tap chuckled. "Lost half your herd, I'll bet. I know that crowd around Baxter Springs."

"They didn't cut Dan's herd," Foley said, "and they didn't turn him aside. Dan took them on through and sold out for a good price."

"Good!" Tap squeezed my shoulder. "We'll make a team, won't we, boy? Man, it's good to be back!"

He glanced over toward the corral where Karen was standing. All of a sudden he said, "Well, you understand what's needed here. When you are ready for the trail, I'll take over."

He walked away from us and went over to where Karen stood by the rail. Tim Foley glanced after him, but his face revealed nothing. Nevertheless, I knew Tim well enough to know he disapproved.

Foley turned and went into the house and the others drifted away, leaving Pa and me standing there together.

"Well," Pa said, "Tap's back. What do you think of him?"

"We're lucky to have him. He knows the waterholes, and he's a good hand. Believe me, Pa, before this drive is over we'll need every man."

"Yes, that we will." He seemed about to say something more, but he did not.

Pa was a canny man and not given to unnecessary talk, and I knew that if he had something on his mind he would say it soon enough. Something was bothering him, however, but all he said a minute later was, "Do you remember Elsie?"

Elsie Henry had been Tap's mother, and I did remember her. She was the only mother I'd ever had, but somehow she never seemed like a mother . . . more like somebody who came to stay for a while and then went away. Yet she was good to Tap and me and, looking back on it, I knew she had done a lot of thinking before she broke loose and ran off.

"Yes, I remember her."

"She wasn't cut out for this life. She should not have come West."

"I often wondered why she did. She was a pretty woman with a taste for pretty clothes and fancy living. Seems to me she would have been happier back East."

"Character," Pa said, "is the thing, whether it's horses, dogs, or men. Or women, for that matter."

He walked off without saying anything more, and I took my horse to the corral and stripped off the outfit and hung it up. All the time I was thinking of what Pa had said, and wondering what lay back of it. Pa had a way of saying things that left a lot unsaid, and I was wondering just how far he wanted that comment to go.

But with the trip coming up, there was very little time for thinking of that. Or of anything else.

It was spring...hot and dry. There had been some good winter rains, and there should be water along the trail to Horsehead Crossing on the Pecos.

Squatting on my heels near the corral, I gave thought to that. Karen and Tap had wandered off somewhere, but right now I was thinking about horses. We would need a cavvy of fifty or sixty head, and with all the horses we could round up between us, including those belonging to Tim Foley and Aaron Stark, we would be short about twenty head.

Two of the wagons needed working on and there was harness to mend. Also, we must get a lot of lead for bullets, and cast enough at least to get us started in case of Comanche trouble. And we would need some additional barrels for carrying water.

Zebony Lambert strolled over and dropped to his heels beside me. He was smoking tobacco wrapped in paper, a habit some of the Texans were picking up from the Mexicans. Most of us smoked cigars, when we smoked.

"So that's Tap Henry."

He spoke in a peculiarly flat tone, and I glanced

around at him. When Zeb spoke in that voice I knew he was either unimpressed or disapproving, and I wanted them to like each other.

"We spent a lot of time together as boys, Zeb. He's my half brother, stepbrother . . . whatever they call it."

"Heard that."

"When his Ma ran off, Pa let him stay on. Treated him like another son."

Zeb looked across the yard to where Tap was laughing and talking with Karen.

"Did he ever see his mother again?"

"No. Not that I know of."

"He fancies that gun, doesn't he?"

"That he does . . . and he's good with it, too."

Zeb finished his cigarette, then pushed it into the dirt. "If you need help," he said, "I stand ready. You'll need more horses."

"You see any wild stuff?"

"Over on the Leon River. You want to try for them?" Zeb was the best wild-horse hunter anywhere around. The trouble was there was so little time. If we wanted to travel when there was water to be found we should be starting now. We should have started two weeks ago.

Zebony Lambert never worked for any man. Often he would pitch in and help out, and he was a top hand, but he would never take pay. Nobody understood that about him, but nobody asked questions in Texas. A man's business and his notions were his own private affair.

"Maybe we can swap with Tom Sandy. There's a lot of young stuff down in the breaks, too young for a trail herd."

"He'll throw in with you if you ask him."

"Sandy?" I could not believe it. "He's got him a good outfit. Why should he move?"

"Rose."

Well, that made a kind of sense. Still, any man who would leave a place like he had for Rose would leave any other place for her, and would in the end wind up with nothing. Rose was a mighty pretty woman and she kept a good house, but she couldn't keep her eyes off other men. Worst of all, she had what it took to keep their eyes on her, and she knew it.

"She'll get somebody killed."

"She'll get Tom killed."

Zeb got up. "I'll ride by about sunup. Help you with that young stuff." He paused. "I'll bring the dogs."

Zebony Lambert had worked cattle over in the Big Thicket and had a bunch of the best cattle-working dogs a man ever did see, and in brush country a dog is worth three cowhands.

He went to his horse and stepped into the saddle. I never tired of watching him do it. The way he went into the leather was so smooth, so effortless, that you just couldn't believe it. Zeb had worked with me a lot, and I never knew a better coordinated man, or one who handled himself with greater ease.

He walked his horse around the corral so he would not have to pass Tap Henry, and just as he turned the horse Tap looked up.

It was plain to him that Lambert was deliberately avoiding him, for around the corral was the long way. Tap laid his eyes on Zeb and watched him ride off, stepping around Karen to keep his eyes on him.

The smell of cooking came from the house, where Mrs. Foley was starting supper.

Karen and Tap were talking when I approached the house. He was talking low and in a mighty persuasive tone, and she was laughing and shaking her head, but I could see she was taken with him, and it got under my skin. After all, Karen was my girl—or so everybody sort of figured.

Tap looked up. "You know, Karen, I can't believe Danny's grown up. He used to follow me around like a sucking calf."

She laughed, and I felt my face getting red. "I didn't follow you everywhere, Tap," I replied. "I didn't follow you over the Brazos that time."

He looked like I'd slapped him across the mouth, but before he could say something mean, Karen put a hand on his sleeve. "You two are old friends...even brothers. Now, don't you go and get into any argument."

"You're right, Karen," I said, and walked by them into the house.

Mrs. Foley glanced up when I came in, and then her eyes went past me to Tap and Karen. "Your brother is quite handsome," she said, and the way she said it carried more meaning than the words themselves.

For three days then we worked sunup to sundown, with Tap Henry, Zeb Lambert, and Aaron Stark working the breaks for young stuff. Pa rode over to have a talk with Tom Sandy about a swap, and Tim Foley worked on the wagons, with his boys to help.

Lambert's dogs did the work of a dozen hands in getting those steers out of the brush and out of the overhang caves along the Cowhouse, which gave the creek its name.

Jim Poor, Ben Cole, and Ira Tilton returned from delivering a small herd to San Antonio and fell in with us, and the work began to move faster.

Every time I had the chance I asked Tap questions about that route west. The one drive I'd made, the one up through Kansas and Missouri into Illinois, had taught me a good deal about cattle, but that was a sight better country than what we were heading into now.

The corn grinding was one of the biggest jobs, and the steadiest. We had a cornmill fixed to a post and two cranks on it. That mill would hold something around a peck of corn, but the corn had to go through two grindings to be right for bread-baking. We ground it once, then tightened the mill and ran it through again, grinding it still finer.

We wanted as much corn ground as possible before the trip started, for we might not be able to use the grinder on the road without more trouble than we could afford. Between grinding the corn and jerking beef, there was work a-plenty for everyone.

None of us, back in those days, wore store-bought clothes. It was homespun or buckskin, and for the most part the men dressed their own skins and made their own clothes, with fringe on the sleeves and pants legs to drain the rain off faster. Eastern folks usually thought that fringe was purely ornamental, which was not true.

For homespun clothes of either cotton or wool, the stuff was carded and spun by hand, and if it was cotton, the seeds were picked out by hand. Every man made his own moccasins or boots, repaired what tools or weapons he had, and in some cases made them from the raw material.

Down among the trees along the Cowhouse the air was stifling. It was a twisty creek, with the high banks under which the cattle took shelter, and it was hot, hard work, with scarcely room to build a loop.

A big brindle steer cut out of the trees ahead of me, and went through them, running like a deer, with me and that steeldust gelding right after him. Ducking a heavy branch that would have torn my head off, I took a smaller one smack across the face, making my eyes water. The steer lunged into a six-foot wall of brush and that steeldust right after him. Head down, I went through, feeling the branches and thorns tearing at my chaps. The steer broke into the open and I took after him, built a loop, and dropped it over his horns.

That old steeldust sat right back on his haunches and we busted that steer tail-over-teakettle and laid him down hard. He came up fighting. He was big, standing over sixteen hands...and he was mad... and he weighed an easy eighteen hundred.

He put his head down and came for me and that steeldust, but that bronc of mine turned on a dime and we busted Mr. Steer right back into the dust again.

He got up, dazed but glaring around, ready for a fight with anything on earth, but before he could locate a target I started off through the brush at a dead run and when that rope jerked him by the horns he had no choice but to come after us.

Once out in the open again and close to the herd, I shook loose my loop and hazed him into the herd.

It was heat, dust, sweat, charging horses, fighting

steers, and man-killing labor. One by one we worked them out of the brush and up onto the plain where they could be bunched. Except for a few cantankerous old mossyhorns, they were usually content as long as they were with others of their kind in the herd.

That tough old brindle tried to make it back to the brush, back to his home on the Cowhouse, but we busted him often enough to make a believer of him.

Tap, like I said, was a top hand. He fell into the routine and worked as hard as any of us.

We rolled out of our soogans before there was light in the sky, and when the first gray showed we were heading for the brush. We wore down three or four horses a day, but there are no replacements for the men on a cow outfit.

Breakfast was usually beef and beans, the same as lunch, or sometimes if the women were in the notion, we had griddle cakes and sorghum...corn squeezings, we called it.

Morning of the third day broke with a lowering gray sky, but we didn't see that until later. We had two days of brutal labor behind us, and more stretching ahead. Usually, I slept inside. Pa and me occupied one side of the Texas, Tim Foley and his family the other side; but with Stark's wife and kids, we gave up our beds to them and slept outside with the hands.

Rolling out of my soogan that third morning, it took me only a minute to put on my hat—a cowhand always puts on his hat first—and then my boots and buckskin pants.

The women had been up and we could hear dishes a-rattling around inside. Tap crawled out of his blankets and walked to the well, where he hauled up a bucket of water and washed. I followed him. He looked sour and mean, like he always did come daybreak. With me it was otherwise—I always felt great in the morning, but I had sense enough to keep still about it.

We went up to the house and Mrs. Foley and Karen filled our plates. That morning it was a healthy slab of beef and a big plate of beans and some fried onions.

Like always, I had my bridle with me and I stuck the bit under my jacket to warm it up a mite. Of a frosty morning I usually warmed it over a fire enough to make it easy for a horse to take, and while it wasn't too cold this morning, I wanted that bronc of mine to be in a good mood.

Not that he would be... or ever was.

We sat on the steps or squatted around on the ground against the wall, eating in silence. Karen came out with the big pot and refilled our cups, and took a mite longer over Tap's cup.

None of us was talking very much, but Zebony moved over beside me when he had finished eating and began to make one of those cigarettes of his.

"You been over to the Leon?"

"No."

"You and me... we take a *pasear* over there. What do you say?"

"There's plenty of work right here," I said. "I don't see—"

"I do," Tap interrupted. "I know what he means."

Zeb touched a delicate tongue-tip to his thin paper. "Do you think," he said to me, "they will let you drive your cattle away?"

"They belong to us."

"Sure—there are mighty few that don't. Those others . . . the newcomers . . . they have no cattle, and they have been living on yours. By now they know you are planning a drive, and are cleaning out the breaks."

"So?"

"Dan, what's got into you?" Tap asked irritably. "They'll rustle every steer they can, and fight you for the others. How many men have we got?"

"Now? Nine or ten."

"And how many of them? There must be thirty."

"Closer to forty," Zeb said. "There's tracks over on the Leon. They are bunching your cows faster than you are, and driving them north into the wild country."

"I reckon we'd best go after them," I said.

Tap got up. "I reckon we had," he said dryly. "And if you ever carried a short gun, you'd better carry one when you go after them."

It made sense. This lot who had squatted around us had brought nothing into the country except some beat-up horses and wagon outfits. Not more than two or three had so much as a milk cow . . . and they had been getting fat on our beef, eating it, which Pa never minded much, and even selling it. And not one of them had done a tap of work. They had come over from the East and South somewhere—a bedraggled bunch of poor whites and the like.

That did not make them easy. Some of that outfit had come down from Missouri and Arkansas, and some were from the Five Counties, where there had been fighting for years. Pa was easygoing and generous, and they had spotted it right off.

"Don't tell Pa," I said. "He's no hand with a gun."

Tap glanced at me briefly as if to say, "And I suppose you are?" But I paid him no mind.

Tim Foley saw us bunched up and he walked over. That man never missed a thing. He minded his own affairs, but he kept an ear to the ground. "You boys be careful," was all he said.

The sun was staining the sky with rose when we moved out from the place. As we rode away, I told Ben Cole to keep the rest of them in the bottoms of the Cowhouse and to keep busy. They knew something was up, but they offered no comment, and we trailed it off to the west, then swung north.

"You know who it is?" I asked Zeb.

"That Holt outfit, Mack, Billy, and Webb—all that crowd who ride with them."

Tough men, and mean men. Dirty, unshaven, thieves and killers all of them. A time or two I'd seen them around.

"Webb," I commented, "is left-handed."

Tap looked around at me. "Now that," he said, "is a good thing to know."

"Carries his gun on the right side, butt first, and he draws with either hand."

We picked up their trail in a coulee near the Leon River and we took it easy. They were driving some twenty head, and there were two men. Following the trail was no trick, because they had made no attempt to hide it. In fact, they seemed to be inviting trouble, and realizing how the odds figured out, they might have had that in mind.

We walked our horses up every slope and looked around before we crossed the ridges or hills. We kept to low ground when we could and just managed to keep the trail in sight.

If we moved our cattle out of this country the rest of that ragtag and bobtail would have to move out or starve to death. Cattle were plentiful in most parts of Texas and it wasn't until later that folks began to watch their beef. For a long time, when a man needed beef he went out and killed one, just as he had buffalo, and nobody paid it no mind.

In those days cattle were good for their hides and tallow, and there was no other market. A few drives had been made to Louisiana, to Shreveport, and over into Alabama, but cattle were a drug on the market. However, this far west the wild cattle had begun to thin out, and fewer were to be found.

This was the frontier, and west of us there was nothing but wide, unsettled country. In those days the settler farthest west in Texas was a farmer who was about four miles west of Fort Belknap, and that was away off north of us, and a little west.

Cattle liked the country farther east or along the river bottoms where the grass was thick. Zeb Lambert told me he had seen a few over on the Colorado, west of us, but they were strays that had somehow found their way there. Nobody lived in that country.

The coolness remained in the morning, clouds were heavy, and there was a dampness as of coming rain. Despite the work we had to do, we hoped for it. Rain in this country meant not only water in the water-holes and basins, but it meant grass on the range. In a few days our lives would depend on both.

Zeb Lambert pulled up. "Dan," he said, "look here."

We both stopped and looked at the trail. Two riders had come in from the east and joined the two we were trailing. The grass was pushed down by their horses' hoofs and had not straightened up—they could have joined them only minutes before.

Tap Henry looked at those tracks. "It could be accident," he said.

"What do you mean?" I asked him.

"Or it could be that somebody told them we were riding this way."

Zebony said nothing, but he started building himself one of those cigarettes he set so much store by.

"Who would do a thing like that?" I asked. "None of our crowd."

"When you've lived as long as me," Tap said shortly, "you won't trust anybody. We were following two men . . . now two more come in out of nowhere."

We rode on, more cautiously now. Tap was too suspicious. None of our folks would carry word to that bunch of no-account squatters. Yet there were four of them now, and only three of us. We did not mind the odds, but it set a man to thinking. If they were tipped off that we were moving against them there might be more of them coming.

Tap suddenly turned his head and saw Zeb cutting off over the rise.

"Now what's got into him?" he demanded.

"He'll be hunting sign. Zeb could track a coon over the cap-rock in the dark of the moon."

"Will he stand?"

"He'll stand. He's a fighter, Tap. You never saw a better."

Tap looked after him, but made no comment. Tap

was riding tall in the saddle this morning, head up and alert, ready for trouble. And Tap Henry was a man who had seen trouble. There had been times before he left us when he had to face up to a difficulty, and no telling how many times since then.

Suddenly, we smelled smoke.

Almost at the same moment we saw our cattle. There must have been three hundred head bunched there, and four men were sitting around the fire. Only one of them got to his feet as we approached.

"Watch it, Tap," I said, "there's more of them."

The hollow where they were was long, maybe a quarter of a mile, and there were willows and cottonwood along the creek, and here and there some mesquite. Those willows shielded the creek from view. No telling what else they might hide.

The remuda was staked out close by. My eyes went to the staked-out horses. "Tap," I said, "five of those horses are showing sweat."

Webb Holt was there, and Bud Caldwell, and a long, lean man named Tuttle. The fourth man had a shock of uncombed blond hair that curled over his shirt collar, and a chin that somehow did not quite track with his face. He had a sour, mean look about him.

"Those cows are showing our brand," I said mildly. "We're taking them back."

"Are you now?" Webb Holt asked insolently.

"And we're serving notice. No more beef—not even one."

"You folks come it mighty big around here," Webb commented. "Where'd you get the right to all these cattle? They run loose until you came along."

"Not here they didn't. There were no cattle here until my father drove them in, and the rest came by natural increase. Since then we've ridden herd on them, nursed them, dragged them out of bogs, and fought the heel-flies and varmints.

"You folks came in here with nothing and you've made no attempt to get anything. We'd see no man go hungry, least of all when he has young ones, so we've let you have beef to eat. Now you're stealing."

"Do tell?" Holt tucked his thumbs behind his belt. "Well, let me tell you something. You folks want to leave out of here, you can. But you're taking no cows."

"If you're counting on that man back in the brush," I said, "you'd best forget him. He won't be able to help you none."

Holt's eyes flickered, and Bud Caldwell touched his tongue to his lips. The blond man never turned a hair. He kept looking at Tap Henry like he'd seen him some place before.

"I don't know what you're figuring on," I said, "but in your place I'd just saddle up and ride out. And what other cattle of ours you have, I'd drive back."

"Now why would we do that?" Holt asked, recovering some of his confidence. "We got the cows. You got nothing. You haven't even got the men."

"The kind we've got," Tap said, "we don't need many."

Holt's eyes shifted. "I don't know you," he said.

Tap jerked his head. "I'm Dan's stepbrother, you might say, and I've got a shooting interest in that stock."

"I know him," the blond man said suddenly. "That's Tap Henry. I knew him over on the Nueces."

"So?"

"He's a gunfighter, Webb."

Webb Holt centered his attention on Tap. He was wary now. Bud Caldwell moved a little to one side, spreading them out. My Patterson revolving rifle lay across my saddle, my hand across the action, and as he moved, I let the muzzle follow him . . . it seemed to make him nervous.

Tap kept his eyes on Holt. We knew there was a man out there in the brush, but we—at least I did—depended on Zeb to take care of him. It was a lot of depending, yet a man can do only so much, and we had four men there in front of us.

"You're going to have a choice to make," Tap said, "any minute now. If you make the right choice, you live."

Webb Holt's tongue touched his lips. He knew he was looking right down the muzzle of Tap's gun, and if Tap was faster than he was, Webb was dead. I had let my horse back up a mite so I could keep both Bud and that blond man under my eyes.

"You can catch up your horses and ride out," I said. "You can start any time you're of a mind to."

Suddenly Zebony Lambert was standing on the edge of the brush. "You boys can open the ball any time you like," he said. "There's nobody out there in the brush to worry about."

You could see them start to sweat. It was three to four now, and my rifle was laid right on one of them. Bud was a tough enough man, but he wasn't going to play the hero. Not on this fine spring morning. Until a few minutes ago he had been complaining the weather was mighty miserable; now any kind of a morning was a fine morning.

"You kill that man?" Holt demanded.

"He didn't make an issue of it," Zeb replied.

Nobody said anything for about a minute, and it was a long minute. Then I stepped my horse up, holding that rifle muzzle on Caldwell.

"Case you're interested," I said, casually, "this here is a Patterson revolving rifle and she shoots five shots....56 caliber."

"Webb...?" Bud Caldwell was kind of nervous. That Patterson was pointed right at his stomach and the range was less than twenty feet.

"All right," Webb Holt replied, "we can wait. We got forty men, and we want these cows. You folks take 'em along now—you won't keep them."

"Webb?" Tap's voice had an edge to it that raised the hair on the back of my neck. "You and me, Webb. Those others are out of it."

"Now see here!" Webb Holt's face was touched with pallor.

"Forty, you said." Tap was very quiet. "I say thirty-nine, Webb. Just thirty-nine."

Bud Caldwell reached for the sky with both hands and the thin man backed up so fast he fell over a log and he just lay there, his arms outspread.

The blond man stood solid where he was. "He called it," he said loudly. "It's them two."

Webb Holt stood with his feet spread, his right side toward Tap Henry. His gun butt was on his right hip, the butt end to the fore and canted a mite.

"Look," he said, "we don't need to—" He grabbed iron and Tap shot him twice through the chest.

"Lucky you warned me about that left hand," Tap said. "I might have made a mistake."

We rounded up those cattle and drove them home, and nobody said anything, at any time.

Me, I was thinking about those other thirty-nine men, and most particularly about Holt's two brothers.

It was time we pulled out, and pulled out fast.

CHAPTER 2

WE WERE THERE when the country was young and wild, and we knew the smell of gunsmoke and buffalo-chip fires. Some were there because they chose the free, wild way, and some were born to it, and knew no other.

To live with danger was a way of life, but we did not think of it as danger, merely as part of all that we must face in the natural order of living. There was no bravado in our carrying of guns, for a man could no more live without a gun in the Texas of the 1850s than he could live without a horse, or without food.

We learned to live like the Indians, for the Indians had been there first and knew the way of the land. We could not look to anyone for help, we must help ourselves; we could not look to anyone for food, we must find our food and prepare it ourselves.

Now there was no more time. Westward the land was open, westward lay our hopes, westward was our refuge. Those were years when half the world grew up with the knowledge that if everything went wrong they could always go west, and the West was foremost in the thinking of all men. It was the answer to unemployment, to bankruptcy, to adventure, to loneliness, to the broken-hearted. It was everybody's promised land.

We pointed the cattle west into the empty land, and

the brindle steer took the lead. He had no idea where he was going, but he intended to be the first one there. Three thousand five hundred head of mixed stuff, with Tap Henry and Pa away out there in front, leading the herd.

The wagons took the flank on the side away from the dust. Tim Foley's boy was driving a wagon, and his wife drove another. Aaron Stark's wife was driving a third, and Frank Kelsey was driving Tom Sandy's big wagon.

Tom and Rose Sandy were coming with us. Zeb Lambert had been right about Sandy, for when he heard of our move he promptly closed a deal on an offer for his ranch, sold all his stock but the remuda and some three hundred head of selected breeding stock, and threw in with us.

He brought two hands with him. Kelsey had been with him ever since Tom Sandy had come to Texas riding a sore-backed mule, and the other hand was Zeno Yearly, a tall Tennessean.

Tilton, Cole, and Poor rode one flank, and two of Pa's other hands, Milo Dodge and Freeman Squires, the other.

We had been making our gather before Tap Henry returned, so getting on the road was no problem. Above all, speed was essential. Now that we had determined to leave, there was no sense in delaying and awaiting an attack, if it came.

We started before sunup, and those first few miles we kept them moving at a trot. We hoped that if we could keep them busy thinking about keeping up they would have less time to worry about where they were going.

We had two scouts out, Tim Foley away on the left, and Aaron Stark to the north, watching for any of the Holt crowd.

Zebony Lambert and me, we ate the dust of the drag, hazing the stragglers back into the herd, changing the minds of any that took a notion to bolt and run for their old home on the Cowhouse.

We made camp fifteen miles out that first night, bedding them down on about six acres in a bottom where the grass was good and there was water from a small stream that flowed toward the Leon River.

Ben Cole and Jim Poor took the first guard, riding around the herd in opposite directions. The rest of us headed for the chuck wagon where the womenfolks had prepared a meal.

From now on, the routine would vary little unless we headed into trouble. We would be lucky to make more than fifteen miles a day with the herd, and most of the time it would be closer to twelve. We were short of horses, having about five horses per man, when a drive of that kind could use anywhere up to eight or nine per man.

A herd of that size would spread out for a mile along a stream when watering, and when bunched for the night would browse a good bit; when actually bedded down they would use a good six acres. After they had fed they would sleep, and about midnight, as if by some secret order, they would rise, stretch, usually browse a little, and finally go back to sleep. Maybe a couple of hours later they would get up again, stretch, and then go back to sleep. Some of them might browse a mite during that second stretch. But by dawn they were all up and ready to move. In ordinary weather two men could keep guard over that many cattle. If there was a storm brewing it might take every hand.

Going to the fire with my cup and a tin plate in my hand, I could hear Ben Cole singing them to sleep. Singing was not just a way of keeping himself company; partly it was that the sound of a human voice—most cowpunchers sounded somewhat less than human when they sang—had a quieting effect. Also, it served notice to the cattle that the shadow they saw out there was a man, and therefore all right.

Karen filled my plate and cup. "You riding all right, Karen?"

She nodded, and her eyes went beyond me to where Tap was sitting. "He's a good man," I said dryly.

Her chin came up defensively. "I like him." Then, she added, "After all, he is your brother."

Taking my grub, I walked over and dropped to the ground where Tap was sitting. "How you coming, kid?" he asked.

After that we ate in silence, and I expect all of us were thinking about what lay behind us as much as about what lay ahead. There were long, dry miles before us, but the season was early, and our chances were good. At least as far as Horsehead Crossing on the Pecos.

When I had cleaned the Patterson, I turned in and stretched out. Nothing better than turning in after a hard day's work. I slept a little away from the rest of them so I could listen better, never wanting anything to come between me and the night.

The clouds had drifted off and the sky was clear. Somewhere over on the bluffs a coyote was talking it up, and from time to time a bird called in the night.

Next thing I knew a hand was shaking me and it was Ira Tilton. He and Stark had relieved Ben Cole and Jim Poor on first guard.

Rolling out, I put my hat on and slid into my boots. Tilton still stood there, chewing tobacco. He started to say something, then turned and walked off toward the fire, which was burned down to coals.

Hitching my chaps, I took the Patterson and went to the fire. Tap, who was sharing my night guard, was already squatting there, cupping his hands around the warm cup, and sipping coffee. He glanced up at me, but said nothing, and neither did I.

Tom Sandy had taken on the job of wrangling horses, and he was up and had a *grulla* caught up for me. Of a right, a hand usually caught up his own mounts, but Tom was not sleeping much these days. Seemed to me Tom should worry less and spend more time in bed, with problems like his.

The night was cold. Glancing at the Dipper, I saw it was after three in the morning. I swallowed another belt of black, scalding coffee and went over to that *grulla* and stepped into the saddle.

He unwound in a tight circle, crow-hopped a few times, and then we started off for the herd, both of us feeling better for the workout.

Tilton had little to say. "Quiet," he said, "quiet so far," and he rode off.

He was a puzzling man in a lot of ways. He had worked for us upwards of three years and I knew him hardly better than when he first came. Not that that was unusual. Folks those days said little about their personal affairs, and many a man in Texas had come there because the climate was not healthy where he came from.

In Texas you did not ask questions about a man's past—that was his business. A man was judged by what he was and how he did what there was to do, and if he had been in trouble elsewhere, nobody paid it any mind. And that went for the law, too, where there was law. The law left you alone, no matter how badly you might be wanted elsewhere, so long as you stayed out of trouble where you were.

As far as that goes, there were several men working for Pa who might have had shady pasts, but they did their work and rode for the brand, and we expected nothing else.

That coyote off on the ridge was talking to the stars. And he was a coyote, too, not an Indian. Once you've heard them both, a body can tell the difference. Only a human voice echoes to any extent, and next to the human the coyote or wolf, but an owl or a quail will not echo at all.

Off across the herd I could hear Tap singing low. He had a good voice, and he was singing "Brennan on the Moor," an old song from the old country about an Irish highwayman. Circling wide, I drew up and listened.

The coyote was still...listening to Tap, most likely...the stars were bright. There was no other sound, only the rustling of the water in the stream nearby.

A big steer stood up and stretched, then another and another. A faint breeze stirred and the big steer lifted his head sharply. Now, a man who trusts to his own hearing only is a fool...you learn not only to look and listen, but to watch the reactions of animals and of birds, for they will often tell you things you would never sense otherwise.

Something was moving out there. That steer faced around, walking a step or two toward the north. My Patterson lifted a mite and I eased back on the hammer. The click was loud in the night, and that big steer flipped an ear at me, but kept his eyes where they were.

Tap was across the herd from me, but he was coming around, walking his horse. The herd was uneasy, so, risking revealing myself to whatever was out there, I commenced talking to them, speaking low and confidently, working my horse in nearer to them.

And I walked my horse toward the trouble.

The big steer kind of ducked his head, and I could almost see his nostrils flare as he moved up a step. He was full of fight, but his attitude puzzled me.

Cattle did not like the smell of Indians, and were apt to get skittish if they came around ... maybe it was the wild smell, or the use of skins so many of them wore, but the herd did not act like they would if Indians were out there.

They would not get excited if a white man was approaching, nor were they as nervous as if it was a bear or a cat. In those days grizzlies often were found down on the plains in Texas, in the Edwards Plateau country, and there were a good many lions around.

Walking that *grulla* ahead, I eased my rifle forward in my hand, then listened.

The big steer had kept abreast of me. He was not frightened, but full of fight. Nevertheless, he liked the company.

And then I heard it.

Straining my ears into the darkness at the edge of the bottom where the cattle were, I heard a faint dragging sound.

It stopped, but after several minutes it began again.

Suddenly, Tap was beside me. "What is it, Dan?" he whispered close to my ear.

"Something dragging. Cover me, Tap. I'm going into the brush for a look."

He caught the reins of my *grulla* when I passed them to him. "Careful, kid. Might be an Indian."

On cat feet, I went into the brush. All my life I'd lived in wild country, and this was second nature to me. Over the years I'd become like any cat, and could move in the night and through the brush making no sound.

A few feet, and then I listened again. Squatting down, I peered under the brush, but it was too dark to see anything. And then I heard that faint dragging sound again, and a panting...a gasping for breath.

Lifting the Patterson, I put the muzzle on the spot and spoke in a low, conversational voice. "You're covered with a five-shot Patterson. If you're in trouble, tell me. Start anything and you get all five shots."

There was a sort of grunt, almost as if somebody tried to speak and couldn't, and then there was no more sound at all.

I eased through the brush and found a long sort of aisle among the willows. There was a faint gray light there, for it was getting on to four o'clock, and lying on the grass was something black.

"Speak up," I said, just loud enough.

No reply. Suddenly there was a faint stirring beside

me and a low growl. It was one of Zeb Lambert's dogs.

"Careful, boy." I whispered it to him, but he was going forward, sniffing and whining.

It was no animal. I knew that. Cautiously I went forward, and suddenly I stood over a dim figure. It was a man, and he was badly hurt.

"Tap?" I called, keeping my voice down. "It's a man, and he's in bad shape!"

"I'll get Milo," he said quickly.

Milo Dodge was a cowhand who'd had a good bit of experience with wounds and such, and one of the best men in any kind of sickness or injury that I'd ever known. On the frontier we were mighty scarce on doctors. In fact, here I was pushing twenty-three and I'd never even seen one, although there was one down to Austin, and I think they had a doctor or two in San Antonio. When sickness came, or wounds, we naturally cared for our own, and had nowhere else to turn.

Seemed like only a minute or two until Milo and Tap were back there, and meanwhile I'd put together a mite of fire to give us light.

The injured man was a Mexican, a slim handsome man with a fine black mustache, but you never did see a man more torn up than he was. His fancy shirt and jacket were soaked with blood and his pants all the way to his knees were covered with blood and soaked with it. He'd dragged himself a long distance, you could see that, but he had a knife in his hand, gripped so hard we couldn't get it loose.

Milo indicated the ripped and torn sleeves of the wounded man's jacket. "Wolves been at him." He pointed at the lacerated condition of the man's wrists.

"He fought them with the knife. Must have had one hell of a time."

"I'll get back to the cattle," Tap said. "You help Milo. Free Squires is out at the herd."

The Mexican stirred and muttered as we cut away his bloody clothing. As we examined him, the story became clear.

Somewhere, several days ago, he had been shot and had fallen from his horse. Obviously his horse had stampeded with him and dragged him at a dead run over the rough country. Somehow the Mexican had held onto his gun long enough to shoot his horse... which was one reason guns were carried, for a man never knew when he might be thrown from one of the half-broken wild horses.

Then he had probably started to crawl, and the wolves had smelled blood and had come after him. He must have used up what ammunition he had, and sometime later they had grown brave enough to rush in on him and he had fought them off with a knife.

"He wants to live," Milo said dryly; "this one really put up a fight."

"I wonder who shot him?"

Milo glanced at me. "I was wondering about that. My bet is that he came from the west."

We heated water and bathed his wounds and his body. The bullet wound and the drag wounds were several days old and some of them were festering. The teeth marks had all come later.

The bullet had gone all the way through him and was pressed against the skin of his back. Milo made a slit with his Bowie knife and took the bullet out. Then he made a poultice of ground maize and bound it on both bullet holes.

It was broad daylight by the time the wounds were dressed, and one of the wagons had pulled alongside to receive the wounded man.

We were the last to move out, for the cattle had already started, and the wagons had all gone but the one into which we loaded the Mexican, bedding him down in the wagon on a mattress Tim Foley had found he could spare.

The day was clear and bright. The cattle had moved off at a good pace with only a few of them striving to turn back.

Lingering behind, I watched them trail off, and then rode my horse up to the highest bluff and looked off across the country. As far as I could see, the grass moved lightly under the wind, and there was nothing else. In the distance a black object moved out of a draw and started into the plain, then another followed ... buffalo.

Searching the plain, I thought I could see the track that must have been made by the Mexican, for grass that is damp does not immediately straighten up when pressed down, and this track had been made, in part at least, during the night.

Holding the Patterson rifle in my right hand, I rode down the slope and scouted the vague track I had seen. Even when I was on the ground and close to the track, it was scarcely visible, nevertheless I found it.

There was blood on the grass.

As I walked the horse along, I saw so much mute evidence of the man's courage that I felt hatred swell within me for whoever had done this to him. Yet I knew that there were many men in Texas, some of them close to me, who believed any Indian or Mexican was fair game.

Whoever the man was, he had come a long way, and he had come with courage, and for that I had only respect. Courage and bravery are words too often used, too little considered. It is one thing to speak them, another thing to live them. It is never easy to face hardship, suffering, pain, and torture. It is always easier to die, simply to give up, to surrender and let the pain die with you. To fight is to keep pain alive, even to intensify it. And this requires a kind of courage for which I had only admiration.

And that Mexican, crawling alone and in darkness, had come a long way, and against fearful odds. I thought of him out there in the darkness, stalked by wolves, close to death, yet fighting back, stabbing, thrusting, fighting with the knife clutched desperately in his fist. This was a man I wanted for a friend, for of his kind there were too few.

Dipping into the coulee, I rode my horse up the other side and followed the herd.

What was it that drove the man on? Was it simply the will to live? To survive in spite of everything? Or was there some other reason? Was it hatred of those who had shot him from the saddle? The desire to live and seek revenge? Or something else?

When I rejoined the herd Pa was working the drag with Zeb.

"Milo says he's in bad shape," Pa said. "Did you see anything?"

"Only that he crawled a long way last night," I said.

The cattle were strung out in a long column, all of half a mile from point to drag. Moving up behind them with Pa, we started bunching them a little more, but keeping them at a good pace. What we wanted now was distance between us and the Cowhouse; and also the faster we got into dry country, the better.

Yet they were settling down, and fewer of them were trying to make a break for their home on the Cowhouse. Nor was there any sign of the Holt crowd or any of that renegade bunch. When nightfall came we had another fifteen miles behind us, and we bedded them down in the shelter of a bluff near the Colorado.

Through dust and rain we made our way westward, and by night the cattle grazed on the short-grass plains and watered from the Colorado River of Texas. Each day with the sun's rising we were in the saddle, and we did not stop until shadows were falling across the land.

The rains were few. Brief showers that served only to settle the dust, but left no pools along the way. The river water ran slack, and Tap's face was drawn with worry when he saw it, but he said nothing, and neither did Pa.

But we had staked everything on this westward move, and all of us knew what lay ahead, and we had all heard of the eighty miles of dry country across which we must take the herd.

It was a hard, grueling business. Alkali dust whitened our faces, dusted over our clothing and our horses. Sweat streaked furrows through the dust, turning our faces into weird masks. Throughout the day the children dropped from the slow-moving wagons to gather buffalo chips for the nighttime fires. These were carried in a hammock of cowhide slung beneath each wagon.

Our trek had taken us north farther than we might need to go, because we wished to strike a known trail sooner, a trail where the difficulties, being known, could be calculated upon and planned for.

We reached that trail below Fort Phantom Hill, and turned south and west again.

We were followed...we saw their dust by day, sensed the restlessness of our horses by night, and we knew they were near.

We did not know whether they were Comanches prowling to steal ponies and take scalps, or whether they were the renegades from the banks of the Brazos and the Cowhouse.

Tap Henry killed a buffalo, and the meat was a welcome thing. Later he killed an antelope, and reported Indian sign. The farther we went, the wilder the country became. We were striking for Horsehead Crossing on the Pecos, used by the Comanches on their raids into Mexico. Named, it was said, for the skulls of the horses that died there after the wild runs up out of Mexico.

Occasionally we found tracks. The old idea that an Indian always rode an unshod horse and a white man a shod one did not hold true, for Indians often stole shod horses from ranches, and the white man often enough rode an unshod pony.

Cracked mud in the bottom of water holes worried us. The river still had water, but it ran shallow. There had been few rains and this was spring—what would it be like in a few weeks more with the sun baking the land?

There was almost a feeling of doom hanging over us that quieted our songs and stilled our voices. The herd was our all. On this move we had staked our futures, perhaps our lives.

Off in the front was Tap, usually riding with Pa, guiding our way through the wild, dry country. At night we heard the wolves. By day occasionally we saw them slinking along, watching for a chance to pull down a calf.

We carried our guns across our saddlebows, and we rode high in the saddle, ready for trouble. Tempers grew short; we avoided each other, each man guarding himself against the hot words that could come too easily under the circumstances.

Karen ignored me. Before Tap returned we had walked out together, danced together, gone riding together. Now I hardly saw her; every moment she could spare she was with Tap.

On this day she was driving the Foley wagon and, breaking away from the herd, I rode over to her. She kept her eyes on the road ahead.

"I haven't seen much of you lately," I said.

Her chin went up. "I've been busy."

"I noticed that."

"I don't belong to you. I don't have to answer to you."

"No, ma'am, you surely don't. And Tap's a good man. One of the best."

She turned and looked right straight at me. "I am going to marry him."

Marry *Tap*? Somehow I couldn't see it. Tap was a drifting man...or that was how I thought of him.

"Didn't take you long to make up your mind," I commented. "You haven't known him a week."

"That's neither here nor there." Her temper flared suddenly. "He's a man! A *real* man! That's more than most people can say! He's more of a man than you'll ever be!"

There did not seem reason to be mad about it, except that she was expecting criticism and was all wound up for it.

"Maybe," I agreed. "Tap's a good man," I said again, "no question about it. Of course, it depends on what makes a man. If I was a woman I'd give a lot of thought to that. Now, Tap is a man's man...he's strong, he's regular, he does his work."

"So?"

"He's like a lot of men, he doesn't like to stay hitched. I don't think he will change."

"You'll see." But her tone was less positive, and I wondered if she had given it any thought at all. Many a time when a girl gets herself involved with romance she is so busy being in love she doesn't realize what it can lead to. They are all in a rosy sort of glow until suddenly they find out the man they love was great to be in love with, but hell to be married to.

Well, I just drifted off, feeling a sort of ache inside me, and angry with myself for it. Seems to me folks are foolish about other people. Karen and I had walked out together, and folks had come to think of her as my girl, but as a matter of fact, we were scarcely more than good friends. Only now that it seemed I'd lost her, I was sore about it. Not that I could ever claim I'd had a serious thought about her, or her about me.

Moving over to the drag, I hazed a laggard steer back into the bunch, and ate dust in silence, feeling mean as a grizzly with a sore tooth.

Yet through it all there was a thread of sanity, and I knew that while there had been nothing between Karen and me but conversation, Tap was all wrong for her. Karen and me had known each other quite a spell, and she knew the others around. Tap Henry was different: he was a stranger who came riding into camp with a fancy outfit and a lot of stories. It was no wonder she was finding something in him that she had been looking for.

Truth to tell, all folks dream, old and young, and they picture in their minds the girl or man they would like to love and marry. They dream great dreams and most of them settle for much less. Many a time a man and wife lie sleeping in the same bed, dreaming dreams that are miles apart and have nothing in common.

Only Tap Henry was a drifter—yet maybe not. Maybe Karen was the answer to his dream, too, and maybe he was going to settle down. It seemed unlikely, but it was none of my business.

Milo Dodge rode back to the drag. "Talked to that Spanish man. He wants to see you."

"Me?"

"You found him. You fetched us to him."

"Where's he from?"

"He won't say. Except he kept asking me about a man with a spider scar on his cheek, a big, dark man with a deep indentation in his cheek and little scars radiating out from it, like a spider's legs."

We made camp on Antelope Creek where the water was clear and sweet. Large oaks and pecan trees grew along the banks, and the place we found to locate was a big open meadow of some thirty or forty acres. The cattle scattered along the creek to drink, then wandered back into the meadow to feed.

Pa came back to where I was sitting my horse in the shade of a big pecan. "Good country," he said. "It tempts a man."

"It does," I said, "and it might be a good thing to hold up here another day and let the cattle fatten up and drink their fill. From now on, according to Tap, the country gets drier and drier."

Tap rode up to join us, and Zeb Lambert followed. The wagons were bunching in a rough circle near the bank of the stream. A faint breeze stirred the leaves of the trees. Tap glanced across the Concho at the bluffs beyond the river. Close to where we sat, the Antelope joined the Concho, and the Concho itself pointed our way west.

"I don't like those bluffs," Tap commented, "but we're as safe here as anywhere, I guess."

Pa told him what we were thinking, and he agreed. We couldn't have chosen a better place to stop, for we had some shelter here from any wind that might blow up, there was good water, and there was grass. The youngsters were already rousing around in the leaves and finding a few pecans left over from the previous fall.

Switching saddles to a lineback dun, I rode over to the wagon where the Mexican was riding. He was propped up a little, and he had some color in his face.

"I'm Dan Killoe," I said.

He held out a slender brown hand and smiled; his teeth were very white. "*Gracias, amigo*. You have save my life, I think. I could go no farther."

"You'd crawled a fair piece. I don't see how you did it."

He shrugged. "It was water I needed, and a place to hide." He grew serious. "*Señor*, I must warn you. By sheltering me you will make the enemy . . . even many enemies."

"A man who makes tracks in this world makes enemies also," I said. "I figure a few more won't matter."

"These are very bad . . . *malo*. They are the Comancheros."

"I've heard of them. Some of your people who trade with the Comanches, is that it?"

"*Si* . . . and we do not approve, *señor*. They found me in their country and they shot at me. I escaped, and they pursued . . . I killed one Comanchero, and one Comanche. Then they hit me. I fell, they caught me with a rope and dragged me. I got out my knife and cut the rope and I took that man's horse from him and rode . . . they pursued again. My horse was killed, but they did not catch me."

This Mexican was something of a man. In my mind's eye I could see that drag and that chase. The only way he could get that horse was to kill its rider, and after that horse was killed he had dragged himself a far piece.

"You rest easy," I told him. "Comanchero or Comanche, nobody is going to bother you."

"They will come for me." He hitched himself to a better position. "You give me a horse and I shall ride. There is no need to risk."

"Let them come." I got down on the ground. "The Good Book says that man is born to trouble. Well, I don't figure on going against the Bible. What trouble comes, we will handle as we can, but nobody in my family ever drove a wounded man from his door, and we aren't about to."

That lineback dun was a running horse. He was also a horse with bottom. Leaving off the work that had to be done, I started for the Concho, and Zeb Lambert fell in alongside me.

This was Indian country, and we were expecting them. We scouted along the river for some distance, mainly hunting tracks, or signs of travel, but we found none.

Across the river we skirted the foot of the bluffs, found a faint trail up, and climbed to the top.

The wind was free up there, and a man could see for a long distance. We sat our horses, looking over the country. Zeb's brown hair blew in the wind when he turned his head to look.

The country away from the river was barren, and promised little. But no matter how we searched the country around we saw no movement, nor any tracks. Finally we circled back to camp.

They were out there somewhere, we were sure of it. But where?

The fires were ablaze when we rode in, and there was the good smell of coffee and of steaks broiling. Ben Cole and Freeman Squires had taken the first guard and were already with the cattle.

The herd was still feeding, relishing the fine, rich grass of the meadow. A few head had returned to the creek to drink again. Somewhere out on the plains a quail called.

Tap Henry came over to where I stood with Pa. "We'd best double the guard tonight," he said. "I've got a feeling."

"We've been lucky so far. The way I see it," Pa said, "that outfit back on the Brazos decided to let us get far enough out so they can blame it on Comanches."

Tap looked around at me. "Who's your Mexican friend?"

"He had trouble with the Comancheros. Says the man after him had a spider scar on his cheek."

Tap gave me an odd look. "Maybe we'd better give him the horse," he said, and then he got up and walked away.

"Now, what's the matter with him?" Pa asked.

It was unlike Tap to say such a thing, or to shy from trouble with anybody. "He must know something we don't," I said. "I'm getting curious about that man with the scar."

We ate, and I caught myself a little shut-eye, spreading my soogan under a pecan tree and lying half awake, half asleep, listening to the bustle around the camp.

All too soon, Zebony came to call me. He was pulling on his boots and, sitting there beside me, he said, "It's quiet out there...too quiet. You better come loaded for bear."

Milo Dodge was at the fire, and so was Aaron Stark. They were drinking coffee, and Stark had his Sharps repeater beside him.

Stamping my feet into my boots, I walked over to the fire. Once I had got to sleep I'd slept sound...so sound it worried me, for I did not like to get into the habit of sleeping so soundly I could not be awakened by the slightest move.

The coffee was strong, and hot as hell. Pa came to the fire and handed me a cold biscuit, which I ate with my coffee.

"You boys be careful, now. I never knew Tap to be jumpy, but he surely is tonight."

Tom Sandy had the lineback dun ready for me, and when I stepped into the saddle I glanced over at Tap's bed. The bed was there, but Tap was not.

"You seen Tap?"

Tom turned away. "No, I haven't!" he said, almost snapping the words at me.

Once we were away from the firelight, the night was dark, for the area was partly shielded by the bluffs and the trees. We rode out together, the four of us, scattering to places about the herd.

At such a time all the little noises of the night become intensely clear, and sounds, which one has always known, are suddenly strange and mysterious. But the ears of men accustomed to the wilderness and the nighttime silences and sounds choose from among the many small noises those which are a warning.

A bird rustling among the leaves, a small animal in the grass, a branch rubbing against another, the grunts and gasps and breathing of the cattle, the click of horns accidentally touching—all these are familiar.

We scattered out, circled, and then fell into pairs. As always, I rode with Zebony.

It was very still. Some of the usual noises we did not hear, and this in itself warned us that something was out there, for the small animals and birds become apprehensive at strange movements among them.

"What do you think, Zeb?"

"They'll try to get close."

Milo Dodge and Stark rode up from the other side. "Milo," I whispered, "Zeb and me, we're going to move out into the edge of the trees. We'll try to meet them before they get to us."

"All right," he said, and watched when I pointed out where we would be.

We never got the chance. There was one brief instant of warning, a rushing in the grass, and then they came with the black loom of the bluff behind them so that we could catch no outline at which to shoot.

They came charging, but in silence, and then the first shot was fired.

It was my shot, fired blindly into the blackness, as much as a warning to the camp as anything.

There was an instant burst of firing in reply, and I heard a heavy fall somewhere near me, and the grunt of a man hitting the ground. A spot of white . . . a man riding a paint horse showed, and I fired again.

The horse swerved sharply and then we were all firing. The surprise had been mutual. They came unexpectedly from the night, but they charged when all four of us were almost together, and our fire smashed them back, caused them to swerve. Shouting and yelling, they bore down on the herd.

The cattle lunged to their feet and stampeded down the valley and away from camp.

Catching the momentary outline of a man against the sky, I fired again, and then again. Hastily I reloaded and started after them. But as suddenly as it had happened, it was over. The attackers were gone and the herd was gone.

Zeb came riding up out of the night. "Dan! *Dan?*"

"Yeah ... somebody's down."

There was a rush of horsemen from camp, and Pa yelled out, "Dan? Are you all right?"

Zeno Yearling spoke from nearby. "Here he is. I think it's Aaron."

Pa struck a light. Aaron was down, all right. He was shot through the chest and he was dead.

"They'll pay for this," Pa said. "By the Lord Harry, they'll pay!"

We circled warily, hunting for other men who were down. We found two of theirs. One was a man named Streeter, a hanger-on who had drifted to the Cowhouse country from over on the Nueces after trouble with the Rangers. The other man we had seen around, but did not know.

"Two for one," Tap said.

"Two, hell!" Pa exploded. "I wouldn't swap Stark for ten of them! He was a good man."

"We'll wait until daylight," I said, "then go hunting."

We rode back to camp with Aaron across a saddle. Nobody was feeling very good about it, and I didn't envy Pa, who would have to tell his widow.

There was no talking around the fire. Picking up some sticks, I built the flames up. We checked around, but nobody else had been hurt.

"Two doesn't seem right," Zeb said. "I know we hit more of them. They came right at us, close range."

Karen and Mrs. Foley were at the fire, making coffee. Taking the Patterson, I cleaned it carefully, checked the loads, and reloaded. Then I went out and looked the lineback dun over to see if he'd picked up any scratches. He looked fit and ready, and I knew him for a tough little horse.

The day broke slowly, a gray morning with a black line of trees that slowly took on shape and became distinct. With the first light, we saddled up again.

Tim Foley, despite his arguments, was forced to stay behind with the wagons, and Frank Kelsey stayed with him.

"You'd better stay, Tom," Pa said. "We've lost one married man already."

"Be damned if I will!" Sandy replied testily. He hesitated. "We should leave another man. Suppose they come back?"

"Free"—Pa looked over at Squires—"you stay. You stood guard last night."

"Now, look here!" Squires protested.

"As a favor," Pa said. "Will you stay?"

Freeman Squires shrugged and walked away. The rest of us mounted up and moved out.

The trail was broad enough, for they had followed the herd into the night, and the herd had taken off into the broad, empty lands to the south.

This was Lipan country, but the Lipans, of late, had been friendly to the white man.

We rode swiftly into the growing light, a tight bunch of armed horsemen, grim-faced and bitter with the loss of Aaron Stark and our cattle. No longer were we simply hard-working, hard-riding men, no longer quiet men intent on our own affairs. For riding after lawless men was not simply for revenge or recovery of property; it was necessary if there was to be law, and here there was no law except what right-thinking men made for themselves.

The brown grass of autumn caught the golden light of morning, and the dark lines of trees that marked the Concho fell behind. Our group loosened, spread out a little to see the tracks better. Among the many cattle tracks we searched for those of riders.

Away off on the flank, I suddenly came upon the tracks of a lone rider whose mount had a magnificent stride. Drawing up, I checked those tracks again.

It was a big horse—far larger and with a better gait than our cow ponies—and it carried a light burden, for the tracks indicated the weight upon the horse must be small.

The tracks came from the northwest, which did not fit with those we followed, unless they were being joined by some scout sent on ahead. Yet why would such a scout be sent? And who among the renegades who followed the Holts could possibly have such a horse?

The tracks had been made the night before, or late the previous afternoon, and I followed them, but kept my own party in sight.

Suddenly the tracks veered sharply west, and I drew rein, looking in that direction.

There was a clump of black on the prairie... mesquite? Cautiously, rifle ready, I walked the dun toward it. The size grew ... it was a clump of trees and brush almost filling a hollow in the plain.

The edge broke sharply off in a ledge of rock, and the tops of the trees barely lifted above its edge. The tracks I followed led to the edge and disappeared into the copse. Warily, I followed.

Then I heard running water, a trickle of water falling into a pool. A wind stirred the leaves, then was still.

My horse, ears pricked, walked into a narrow trail where my stirrups brushed the leaves on either side. After some thirty yards of this, there was a sudden hollow under the arching branches of the live oaks, and an open space some fifty feet in diameter, a pool a dozen feet across, and a magnificent black horse that whinnied gently and pricked his ears at my dun. There was coffee on a fire, and bacon frying, and then a voice spoke, "Stand where you are, *señor,* or I shall put a bullet where your breakfast is."

My hands lifted cautiously. There was no mistaking the ominous click of the cocking gun . . . but the voice was a woman's voice.

CHAPTER 3

SHE WAS YOUNG and she was lovely, and the sun caught and entangled itself in the spun red-gold of her hair, but the rifle in her hands was rock-steady, its muzzle an unwinking black eye that looked at my belt buckle.

A flat-crowned Spanish hat lay upon her shoulders, held by the chin strap, which had slipped down about her throat. She was dressed in beautifully tanned buckskin, the skirt was divided for easy riding—the first I had seen, although I'd heard of them before this.

"Who are you? Why are you following me?"

"Unless you're one of the cow thieves that ran off our herd last night, I wasn't following you until I came across your tracks out there."

The rifle did not waver, nor did her eyes. "Who are you? Where do you come from?"

As she talked, I was getting an idea. Maybe a wild one, but an idea.

"The name is Dan Killoe, and we're from over on the Cowhouse. We're driving to New Mexico. Maybe to Colorado. We're hunting new range."

"You spoke of cow thieves."

"They ran our herd off last night. The way we figure, it's a passel of thieves from back on the Cowhouse. If we leave the country with our stock, they've all got to go to work."

She watched me with cool, violet eyes. Yet it seemed to me she was buying my story.

"You must have heard the cattle go by a couple of hours back," I added. "Now may I put my hands down?"

"Put them down. Just be careful what you do with them."

Carefully, I lowered them to the horn of the saddle. Then I glanced around. "Seems to me you're a long way from home," I said, "and you a woman alone."

"I am not alone," she said grimly. "I have this." She gestured meaningfully with her rifle.

"That's a mighty fine horse you've got there. Fact is"—I pushed my hat back on my head—"that's one reason I followed you. I wanted to see that horse."

She lowered her rifle just a little. "Have some coffee?" she suggested. "It will boil away."

Gratefully, I swung down. "I'd like a cup. Then I'll have to follow after the others and lend a hand. I figure in about an hour we're going to have us a scrap with those thieves."

My own cup hung to my saddle horn and I helped myself and looked again at her. Never in all my born days had I seen a girl as pretty as that.

"Now," I said, "I've got an idea. You wouldn't be looking for somebody, would you?"

She glanced at me quickly. "Why do you ask that?"

"Wondered." I took a swallow of hot coffee. "Do you know anything about the Comancheros?"

Oh, I'd hit pay dirt all right, that was plain enough from the way she reacted. "I know about them," she said.

"We picked up a maverick a while back, and he was

in mighty bad shape. He had been shot and he had been dragged, and the Comancheros had done it."

"He's alive? He's all right?"

"Friend of yours?"

"Where is he? I am going to him."

"He's in bad shape, so you take it easy. We found him out in the brush, and the wolves had been at him. He'd fought them off, but he was chewed up some." I swallowed the last of the coffee and rinsed my cup at the stream. "He's got nerve enough for three men. How he ever crawled so far, I'll never know."

She gathered her meager gear. "I am going to him. Where is your camp?"

"Ma'am, that boy is in bad shape and, like I said, he had some rough treatment. I don't know you, and for all I do know you might be one of his enemies."

"I am his adopted sister. After my father was killed, his family took me into their home."

It was time I was getting on, for I'd already lost too much time, and the Kaybar outfit was riding into trouble. "You ride careful when you get to camp. They are expecting trouble, and you might collect a bullet before they see you.

"You ride north from here. The camp is on the Antelope near where it empties into the Middle Concho. Tell them Dan Killoe sent you."

Mounting up, I rode up to the plain and swung south. Keeping to low ground, I rode swiftly along, coming up only occasionally to look for the trail of torn earth where the Kaybar crew had passed.

They had been moving slowly, so I figured to overtake them before they ran into trouble. But I was almost too late.

When I finally saw them they were fanned out, riding toward a bluff. The country beyond that bluff stretched out for miles, and I could catch glimpses of it. Suddenly, just as I slowed down so as not to rush among them, the grass stirred between them and me and a man reared up, rifle in hand.

Intent upon making a kill, he did not notice me, and my horse made little sound with his hoofbeats on the plain's turf. Not wishing to stampede their horses by rushing among them, the dun was walking at a slow pace when the man rose from the brush.

He came up with his rifle and lifted it, taking a careful sight on Tap, and I slapped the spurs to the dun. I was not a rider who used his spurs, and the startled dun gave one tremendous leap and then broke into a dead run.

The ambusher heard the sound of hoofs too late, and even as he brought the rifle into position to fire, he must have heard that rushing sound. It could not have been loud, for the turf was not hard and there was short grass, but he turned quickly, suddenly, but I was fairly on top of him and he had no chance. I fired that Patterson of mine like you'd fire a pistol, gripping it with one hand and holding it low down close to my thigh.

He was slammed back by that .56-caliber bullet as though struck by an axe, and then I was over and past him and riding up to join the others.

As if on order, they all broke into a run, and when I reached the ridge they had been mounting, I saw the camp that lay below.

At least two dozen men were lying about, and my shot must have startled them, for they evidently had jumped up and started for their guns, those who didn't have them alongside.

There were several men with the herd, and my first shot went for the nearest guard. It was a good shot, for he left the saddle and tumbled in a heap, and then we ripped into that camp.

We were outnumbered two to one, but our coming was a complete surprise and we made the attack good. I saw Tap wheel his horse and come back through a second time, blasting with a six-shooter. Then he tucked that one away and started blasting with a second one, and unless I missed my guess, Tap would be carrying at least two more.

In those days of cap-and-ball pistols many a man when fighting Indians—and some outlaws, too—carried as many as six pistols into action because of the time it took to reload. And some carried extra cylinders that could be placed fully loaded into the pistol.

A big man with a red beard and red hair all over his chest jumped at me, swinging a rifle that must have been empty. The dun hit him with a shoulder and knocked him head over heels into the fire.

He let out an awful yell and bounded out of that fire with his pants smoking, and sticks and coals were scattered all over the place.

We swept on through camp and started those cattle hightailing it back to the north, and if we picked up a few mustangs in the process, we weren't taking time to sort them out, even if we'd been a mind to.

We got off scot-free.

Ben Cole had a bullet burn alongside his neck, and he grumbled all the way back to the Concho about it. Fact is, it must have smarted something fierce, with sweat getting into it, and all. But you'd have thought he had a broken knee or a cracked skull, the way he took on.

Zeno Yearly rode back alongside me. He was a long-legged man with a long face, and he didn't look like he could move fast enough to catch a turtle in a barley field. However, out there when the fighting was going on, I'd noticed he was a busy, busy man.

Tap fell back beside me. "Where'd you drop off to?" he asked. "I figured you'd taken out, running."

"Had to stop back there to talk to a girl," I said carelessly. "She offered me coffee, so I stopped by."

He looked at me, grinning. "Boy, any girl you find out in this country, you can have!"

"Prettiest girl you ever did see," I commented, "and she'll be back at camp when we get there."

"You're funnin'!" He stared at me, trying to make out what I was getting at. The idea that the girl actually existed he wouldn't consider for a moment, and in his place I wouldn't have believed it either.

"Too bad you're getting married," I said. "Puts you out of the running."

His face flushed. "Who said I was getting married?" he demanded belligerently.

"Why, Karen. She allowed as how you two were looking for a meeting house."

His face flushed a deeper red under the brown. "Nothing to that," he protested. "Nothing to that, nothing at all."

"She seemed mighty positive," I said, "and you know how folks out here are, when it comes to trifling with a good woman. Tim Foley is a mighty handy man with a shotgun, Tap. I'd ride careful, if I were you."

He grinned. He was recovering himself now. "Now, don't you worry, boy. Nobody ever caught old Tap in a bind like that. Karen's a fine girl . . . but *marriage*? I ain't the marrying kind."

Whether it was what I'd said or something else, I can't say, but that night I noticed Karen sitting by herself, and she wasn't liking it, not one bit.

The red-headed girl was there, and she was the center of quite a bit of fuss by the womenfolks. Most of the men hung back. She was so beautiful it made them tongue-tied, not that any of them, unless it was Tap, would have won any prizes in an elocution contest.

Me, I hadn't anything to say to her. She was the prettiest girl I'd ever seen, and to ride out there by herself took a lot more nerve than most men would have, riding right through the heart of Comanche country, like that.

Two or three times she looked over at me, but I paid her no mind. Most of the time she spent talking to the Mexican or fixing grub for him.

Karen's face was pale and her lips were thin. I'd never noticed how sharp and angular her face could get until that night, and I knew she was mad, mad clean through. Tap, he just sat and joked with the men, and when he got up Karen would have cut him off from the bunch, but he stepped into the saddle and rode out to the herd.

Tom Sandy came up to the fire for more coffee, and for the first time I saw he was wearing a six-shooter. He favored a rifle, as I do, but tonight he was packing a gun. Rose was at the fire, too. A dark, pretty woman with a lot of woman where it mattered, and a way of making a man notice. She had those big dark eyes, and any time she looked at an attractive man those eyes carried a challenge or an invitation. Or something that could be taken that way. Believe me, she was no woman to have around a cow outfit.

Sandy looked across the fire at her a few times, and he looked mean as an old razorback boar.

Rose dished up some beans and beef for Tom and brought them to him, and then she turned to me. "Dan, can I help you to something?"

I looked up at her and she was smiling at me, and I swallowed a couple of times. "Thank you, ma'am. I would like some more of those *frijoles*."

She went to the fire for them, giving her hips that extra movement as she walked away, and Tom Sandy was staring at me with a mean look in his eye.

"Hot," I said, running a finger around my shirt collar.

"I hadn't noticed," he said.

Pa came over and dropped down beside me. "Tap figures we'd better get on the road right away in the morning, before daybreak. What do you think?"

"Good idea," I said.

Tom Sandy walked off, and Pa looked at me. "Dan, you aren't walking out with Rose Sandy, are you?"

"Are you crazy?"

"Somebody is. Tom knows it and he's mad. If he finds out, there'll be a killing."

"Don't look at me. If I was planning to start something like that, she wouldn't be the one."

At sunup we were well down the trail and moving steadily westward. Away from the stream the land was dry and desolate, and showed little grass. It was a warning of what lay ahead.

So far we had done well. Despite the driving off of our cattle and our recovery of them, we seemed to have lost none, and we had gained by half a dozen horses that had been driven off with the cattle when we recovered them.

We saw little game. There were the usual prairie dogs and jackass rabbits, and when we camped that night Zeno caught us a mess of catfish, which offered a change of diet.

Out on the plains away from the river there was prickly pear, greasewood, and sagebrush, but mighty little else. Here and there in a bottom or at a creek crossing we found a few acres of grama, and we took time out to let the cattle eat. It was a scary thing to think of the long marches ahead of us with grass growing less and less.

We all knew about the eighty miles of dry march ahead of us, but we preferred not to think of it. Each night we filled our barrels to have as much water as we could for the day to come. But all of us knew there might be a time when there would be no water, not even for ourselves and our horses.

We nooned at a pool, shallow but quite extensive, but when we left, it was only a patch of muddy earth churned by the feet of our cattle.

While there, I went up to the Mexican's wagon to see how he was . . . or at least, that's what I told myself.

When I spoke, the redhead drew back the curtain, and her smile was something to see. "Oh, please come in! Miguel has been telling me how it was you who found him."

"Just happened to be first," I said, embarrassed.

"If you had not found me," Miguel said, "I should

now be dead. That I know. Nobody else had come to see what lay out there, even if they heard me."

"Your name is Dan Killoe?" she asked. "I am Conchita McCrae. My father was Scotch-Irish, my mother a Mexican."

"You had nerve," I said. "You must have ridden for days."

"There was no one else. Miguel's father is dead, and there is only our mother . . . his mother. She is very old, and she worried about her son."

Well, maybe so, but it took nerve for a girl—or a man for that matter—to ride into Comanche country alone. Or even to drive through it, as we were. She had a fast horse, but that isn't too much help when the Comanche knows the country and is a master at ambuscade. There was very little about hunting or fighting that the Indian did not know, and what he did not know, he learned fast.

Conchita McCrae stood tall in my estimation, and I liked the way she looked straight into your eyes and stood firmly on her small feet. That was more of a woman than I had ever seen before.

"The Comancheros," Miguel said, "I do not approve of what they do. They are some of my people who trade with the Comanche, and it is a profitable trade, but they sell the rifles with which to kill, and they kill our people, and yours also."

He paused to catch his breath, and then said, speaking more slowly, "They believed I was spying when I was only hunting wild horses, for they knew me as one who did not approve. I had hoped to avoid trouble with them, but there are men among the Comancheros who are worse than the Comanches themselves."

"The man with the scar?"

The skin around his eyes seemed to draw back. "He is the worst of them. He is Felipe Soto. You know of him?"

I knew of him. He was a gunfighter and a killer. It was said he had killed more than twenty men in hand-to-hand battles with knife or gun. How many he had killed in fights of other kinds, no man could guess.

In a few short years the man had become a legend, although so far as I knew he had appeared east of the Pecos on only one occasion. He had crossed the Rio Grande from Matamoras and killed a man in Brownsville.

He was an outlaw, but he was protected by many of his own people, and among them he had been guilty of no crimes. A big man, he was widely feared, and even men who might have faced him with some chance of winning did not care to take the risk such a meeting would involve.

"Where did they find you?"

"Ah! There is the trouble, *amigo*! They find me just as I have come upon their . . . shall we say, rendezvous? It is a word you know?

"There is a canyon to the north, a great long, high-walled canyon, and in the bottom there is rich, green grass. They were there . . . the Comanches and the Comancheros. This place I have seen is a secret place, but I had heard of it. It is the Palo Duro Canyon."

"They will follow him, Mr. Killoe," Conchita said. "They will not let him live now. The Comancheros are men of evil. If they do not find him now, they will come searching for him when he is home again."

"What they do then is no business of mine," I said,

"but we won't let him be taken from us. I promise you that."

There was a movement behind me. "Don't make any promises you can't keep."

It was Tap Henry. His features were hard, and there was a kind of harsh impatience in his eyes that I had seen there before this.

"I'll keep the promise, Tap," I replied quietly. "I have made the promise, and it will stick."

"You'll listen to me," Tap replied shortly. "You don't know what you are walking into."

"I have made my promise. I shall keep it."

"Like hell you will!" Tap's tone was cold. "Look, kid, you don't know what you're saying."

He paused, taking a cigar from his pocket. "We've got enough to do, getting our cattle west, without borrowing trouble."

"Please," Miguel had risen to one elbow, "I wish no trouble. If you will loan me a horse, we can go."

"Lie down, *señor*," I said. "You are my guest, and here you will stay."

"Who's leading this outfit, you or me?"

"I thought Pa was," I said dryly. "When it comes to that, we're both working for him."

His face stiffened a little. "Well, we'll see what Pa has to say, then!" he said sarcastically.

We walked together toward where Pa stood by the fire. Zeb Lambert was there, squatting on his heels, and Zeno Yearly was there, too. Ira Tilton had come in from his guard for coffee and I saw his eyes go quickly to Tap Henry.

"Pa," Tap said, "the kid here has promised those Mexicans that they can have our protection all the way into New Mexico. Now, we know the Comancheros are hunting them, and that means trouble! They can muster fifty, maybe a hundred white men and more Comanches, and we're in no shape to stand up to that kind of a crowd. I say we let them shift for themselves."

Zeno glanced up at Tap, but his long horse-face revealed nothing.

Pa glanced at me. "What do you say about this, Dan?"

"I told them they were our guests, and they were safe with us."

Pa looked at Tap. "What's wrong with that?"

Tap's face darkened, and his eyes were cold. "Pa, you don't know what you're saying. Neither you nor the cattle nor any of us will get through if that outfit tackles us! I heard that Mex say he knew where their hideout was, and that's the best-kept secret in this part of the country. They dasn't let him live."

"We will try to see that he does," Pa said quietly.

Pa was a square-faced man with carefully combed gray hair and a trimmed gray mustache. No matter how bad times got or how busy we were, Pa was always shaved, his hair was always trimmed. And I do not recall ever seeing Pa lean on anything—he always stood on his own two feet.

He looked steadily at Tap now. "I am surprised, Tap. You should know that I would never leave a man—least of all a man and a woman—out here on the plains alone. If we have to fight to protect them, then we shall have to fight."

Tap Henry stared at him with sullen eyes. "Pa, you can't do that. These folks are nothing to you. They are—"

"We took them in. They needed help. So long as I live, they will have it from me. I have never turned a man from my door, and I never shall."

Tap Henry drew a deep breath. "Pa..." He was almost pleading. "These Comancheros...they're worse than Comanches. Believe me, I know—"

"How do you know, Tap?" Pa asked mildly.

Tap shut up and turned sharply away. That he believed us all to be a pack of fools was obvious, and maybe he was right. Pa was not a man who ever preached to anyone, least of all to his boys, but he had taught us always to stand on principle. I say taught us, but it was mostly example. A man always knew where Pa Killoe stood on any question, and no nonsense about it.

Not that we had any doubts about the trouble we were in. The plains were alive with Comanches, and the Comancheros were as bad, if not worse, and Tap was right—they would be hunting Miguel.

An idea that was sheer inspiration came to me of a sudden. More than likely they already believed Miguel to be dead, but suppose they wanted to see the body before they believed?

"Pa...I think we should bury him. Miguel, I mean."

Pa glanced around at me; and Conchita, who had come down from the wagon, stood stock-still, listening. "We should bury him right here," I said, "and put a marker over the grave."

Zeno Yearly walked over to the wagon and took a shovel from the straps that bound it to the wagonside where it would be handy. Without any further talk, he walked off to one side and stuck the spade into the ground. Getting another shovel, I joined him.

We dug the grave four feet deep then dropped in a layer of big rocks, then another. If they were curious enough to open the grave they might not be curious enough to lift out all those rocks. We filled in the dirt and put up a marker.

"Name?" Yearly asked.

"No," I said, "we don't want them to think he talked. Just make it: *Unknown Mexican Died on This Spot April 16, 1858.*"

After a short nooning, we rolled our wagons again, and the herd moved on.

Tap had nothing to say, but he was short-tempered as a rattlesnake in the blind, which is the way they refer to a snake when he is shedding his skin. At that time a rattler won't rattle—he simply strikes at anything that moves.

But Tap was wary. He rode far out much of the time, scanning the hills. The word got around, of course, and most of the hands went out fully armed and loaded for bear. We kept the herd moving late, and five miles farther on we crossed the South Fork, sometimes called the Boiling Concho. This was real water—deep, clear, and quite rapid in some places, and the herd spread out along the banks for water while we hunted a place to ford it.

Tap found the spot he was looking for—a ledge of rock under the water that gave sure footing for the cattle and was wide enough to take two wagons abreast. We crossed over, moving them slow, and started across some flat country dotted with mesquite and occasional live oak. The grass was good. We crossed Dove Creek, filled with rushes, and pushed on to Good Spring Creek.

The water was clear and cold, the grass good, and there was plenty of wood and buffalo chips. It was coming on to dark when we rounded the cattle into position and circled our few wagons.

Zeno Yearly got out his tackle and threw a bait into the creek. By the time the sun was gone he had six black bass, all of them good. Those fish were so hungry and so unfamiliar with fishhooks that they could scarcely wait to grab.

The fish tasted good. Nobody was saying anything but our grub wasn't holding up like we had hoped. We had figured to kill more game, and we just hadn't seen any, and we didn't want to kill a steer because we would need all we had. Aside from the steers, we were depending on the rest for breeding stock.

Nobody talked very much, and we ate quickly and turned in for a rest. Ben Cole and Zeno Yearly took the first guard, but Tap Henry was awake, too. He smoked near the fire for a while, then got up and walked out beyond the wagons. He was still standing out there alone when I dropped off to sleep.

Tom Sandy woke me. He looked thinner, and he was rough waking me. I got out of my blankets into the cool night and put on my hat, then my boots. Tom had walked off to the fire without saying anything, but he looked mean and bitter.

Zebony was at the fire, and he glanced up at me. "Did you see Tom?"

"I saw him."

"Trouble's riding that man. Something's chewing on him."

Glancing over at Tap's bed, I saw him there, sleeping. We mounted up and rode by and out to the herd. We were relieving Kelsey and Squires.

"Quiet," Kelsey said.

They rode off toward the fire and Zebony started away. From where I sat by the edge of the herd I could see Tom Sandy huddled in his blankets near the wagon. My eyes strayed to Tap's bed, but somehow it did not seem occupied. Bushes obscured it somewhat, however, and it was none of my affair.

Slowly, I started around the herd. I was riding a big roan horse that was hard-riding but powerful, and for his size, quite fast.

My mind went suddenly to the blond gunman who had accompanied Webb Holt on the day Tap killed him. That man worried me. He had taken the whole affair too calmly, and I had a feeling we would see more of him. And Bud Caldwell, too, for that matter.

It was almost an hour later and the cattle had gotten to their feet for a stretch, and some had begun to graze a little, when suddenly a big longhorn's head came up sharply. Looking where he looked, I saw only the blackness of a patch of live oak.

With the Patterson ready in my hand, I walked the roan toward the trees. Trust a longhorn to spot trouble, for although they were considered domestic cattle, actually they were wild things, reacting like wild things, and most of them lived wild all their lives.

Suddenly, from the corner of my eye, I saw movement in the blackness, and caught a gleam of light on a gun barrel.

Somebody else was searching that patch of woods, somebody from our camp. Stepping the roan around a patch of brush, I took him into the darkness. He was curious, and he could sense danger as any mustang would, so he stepped light and easy.

There was a stir of movement, a low murmur of voices and then a woman's soft laugh.

An instant there, I stopped. I could feel the flush climb up my neck, for I knew what I would find in there ... and in the same instant I knew who that other man was.

Instantly, I pushed the roan through the brush. It crackled, and I saw the man across the small clearing lift his rifle. Slapping spurs to the roan, I leaped him ahead and struck up the gun before it could be fired. Grasping the barrel, I wrenched it from the hands of the startled man.

There was a gasp of alarm, and then a cool voice said, "Turn him loose, boy. If he wants to come hunting me, give him his chance."

"Give me the rifle, Dan." It was Tom Sandy. Only he was not the easygoing man I had known back on the Cowhouse. This was a cold, dangerous man.

"Give me the rifle," Sandy persisted. "I shall show him what comes to wife-stealers and thieves."

"Let him have it," Tap said coolly.

Instead I laid my rifle on Tap. "You turn around, Tap, and you walk back to the herd. If you make a move toward that gun, I'll kill you."

"Are you crossing me?" He was incredulous, but there was anger in him, too.

"We will have no killing on this outfit. We've trouble enough without fighting among ourselves." I saw Tom Sandy ease a hand toward his shirtfront where I knew he carried a pistol. "Don't try it, Tom. That goes for you, too."

There was silence, and in the silence I saw Rose Sandy standing against a tree trunk, staring at the scene in fascinated horror.

Others were coming. "Turn around, Tom, and walk back to camp. We're going to settle this, here and now. You, too, Rose."

She looked up at me. "Me?" Her voice trembled. "What—?"

"Go along with him."

Tap Henry stood watching me as they walked away. "You'll interfere once too often, boy. I'll forget we grew up together."

"Don't ever do it, Tap. I like you, and you're my brother. But if you ever draw a gun on me, I'll kill you."

The late moon lit the clearing with a pale, mysterious light. He stood facing me, his eyes pinpoints of light in the shadow of his hat brim.

"Look, you damned fool, do you know who you're talking to? Have you lost your wits?"

"No, Tap, and what I said goes as it lays. Don't trust your gun against me, Tap, because I'm better than you are. I don't want to prove it...I don't set store over being called a gunfighter like you do. It's a name I don't want, but I've seen you shoot, Tap, and I can outshoot you any day in the week."

He turned abruptly and walked back to camp. Pa was up, and so were the others—Tim Foley and his wife, Karen, her face pinched and tight, and all of us gathering around.

"Free," I said to Squires, "ride out and take my place, will you? We've got a matter to settle."

Pa was standing across the fire in his shirtsleeves, and Pa was a man who set store by proper dress. Never a day but what he wore a stiff collar and a necktie.

Tap walked in, a grin on his hard face, and when he looked across at Tom Sandy his eyes were taunting. Tom refused to meet his gaze.

Rose came up to the fire, holding her head up and trying to put an impudent look on her face and not quite managing it.

Pa wasted no time. He asked questions and he got answers. Tap Henry had been meeting Rose out on the edge of camp. Several times Tom Sandy had managed to see them interrupted, hoping Rose would give up or that Tap would.

Karen stood there listening, her eyes on the ground. I knew it must hurt to hear all this, but I could have told her about Tap. As men go he was a good man among men, but he was a man who drew no lines when it came to women. He liked them anywhere and he took them where he found them and left them right there. There would have been no use in my telling Karen more than I had ... she would believe what she wanted to believe.

Worst of all, I'd admired Tap. We'd been boys together and he had taught me a good deal, but we were a team on this cow outfit, and we had to pull together if we were going to make it through what lay ahead. And every man jack on the drive knew that Tap Henry was our insurance. Tap had been over the trail, and none of us had. Tap knew the country we were heading toward, and nobody else among us did.

Tap was a leader, and he was a top hand, and right now he was figuring this was a big joke. The trouble was, Tap didn't really know Pa.

Tom Sandy had heard Rose get out of the wagon, and he knew that Tap was gone from his bed, so he followed Rose. If it hadn't been for that old longhorn spotting something in the brush, Sandy would have unquestionably killed one of them, and maybe both. He would have shot Tap where he found him. He said as much, and he said it cold turkey.

Tap was watching Sandy as he talked, and I thought that Tap respected him for the first time. It was something Tap could understand.

"What have you to say for yourself?" Pa asked Tap.

Tap Henry shrugged. "What can I say? He told it straight enough. We were talking"—Tap grinned meaningly—"and that was all."

Pa glanced over at Rose. "We're not going to ask you anything, Rose. What lies between you and your husband is your business. Only this: if anything like this happens again, you leave the drive...no matter where we are. Tom can go or stay, as he likes."

Pa turned his attention back to Tap. His face was cold. "One thing I never tolerate on my drives is a troublemaker. You've caused trouble, Tap, and likely you'd cause more. I doubt if you and Tom could make it to the Pecos without a killing, and I won't have that, nor have my men taking sides."

He paused, and knowing Pa and how much he cared for Tap, I knew how much it cost him. "You can have six days' grub, Tap, and a full canteen. You've got your own horse. I want you out of camp within the hour."

Tap would not believe it. He was stunned, you could see that. He stood there staring at Pa like Pa had struck him.

"We can't have a man on our drive, which is a family affair, who would create trouble with another man's wife," Pa said, and he turned abruptly and walked back to our wagon.

Everybody turned away then, and after a minute Tap walked to the wagon and began sorting out what little gear he had.

"Sorry, Tap," I said.

He turned sharp around. "Go to hell," he said coldly. "You're no brother of mine."

He shouldered his gear and walked to his horse to saddle up. Ira Tilton got up and walked over to him, and talked to him for a minute, then came back and sat down. And then Tap got into the saddle and rode off.

Day was breaking, and we yoked up the wagons and started the herd. The river became muddy and shallow. We let the cattle take their time, feeding as they went, but the grass was sparse and of no account.

We had been shorthanded when we started west, and since then we had buried Aaron Stark and lost Tap Henry. It wasn't until the wagons were rolling that we found we had lost somebody else.

Karen was gone.

She had slipped off, saddled her pony, and had taken off after Tap.

Ma Foley was in tears and Tim looked mighty grim, but we had all seen Tap ride off alone, and so far as anybody knew he had not talked to Karen in days. But it was plain enough that she had followed him off, and a more fool thing I couldn't imagine.

Pa fell back to the drag. "Son, you and Zeb take out and scout for water. I doubt if we will have much this side of the Pecos. There's Mustang Ponds up ahead, but Tap didn't say much about them."

We moved out ahead, but the land promised little. The stream dwindled away, falling after only a few miles to a mere trickle, then scattered pools. Out on the plains there was a little mesquite, all of it scrubby and low-growing. The few pools of water we saw were too small to water the herd.

The coolness of the day vanished and the sun became hot. Pausing on a rise where there should have been a breeze, we found none. I mopped my neck and looked over at Zebony.

"We may wish we had Tap before this is over."

He nodded. "Pa was right, though."

At last we found a pool. It was water lying in a deep hole in the river, left behind when the upper stream began to dry out, or else it was the result of some sudden, local shower.

"What do you think, Zeb?"

"Enough." He stared off into the distance. "Maybe the last this side of Horsehead." He turned to me. "Dan, that Pecos water is alkali. The river isn't so bad, but any pools around it will kill cattle. We've got to hold them off it."

Suddenly he drew up. On the dusty earth before him were the tracks of half a dozen unshod ponies, and they were headed south. The tracks could be no more than a few hours old.

"As if we hadn't trouble enough," Zeb commented.

He squinted his eyes at the distance where the sun danced and the atmosphere shimmered.

Nothing...

"I wonder what became of Tap?"

"I've been wondering if that Foley girl caught up with him," Zeb said. "It was a fool thing for her to do." He glanced around at me. "Everybody thought you were shining up to her."

"We talked some...nothing to it."

We rode on. Sweat streaked our horses' sides and ran down under our shirts in rivulets. The stifling hot dust lifted at each step the horses took, and we squinted our eyes against the sun and looked off down over the vast empty expanse opening before us.

"If the women weren't along..." I said.

We had come a full day's drive ahead of the herd, and there was water back there, water for a day and a night, perhaps a little more, but ahead of us there was no sign of water and it was a long drive to Horsehead Crossing.

"We'll lose stock." Zeb lit a cigarette. "We'll lose a-plenty, unless somewhere out there, there's water."

"If there is, it will be alkali. In the pools it will be thick, and bad enough to kill cattle."

Removing my hat to wipe the hatband, I felt the sun like a fire atop my skull—and I carry a head of hair, too.

Once, dipping into a hollow, we found some grass. It was grama, dead now and dry, but our horses tugged at it and seemed pleased enough.

From the rim of the hollow we looked again into the distance toward Horsehead.

"Do you suppose there's another way to drive?" I asked.

Zeb shrugged. "It ain't likely." He pointed. "Now, what do you think of that?"

In the near distance, where the road cut through a gap in the hills, buzzards circled. There were only two or three of them.

"First living thing we've seen in hours," Zeb commented. "They must have found something."

"If they found anything out there," I said, "it's dead, all right."

We walked on, both of us shucking our firearms. I held the Patterson with light fingers, careful to avoid the barrel, which was hot enough to burn.

The first thing we saw was a dead horse. It had been dead all of a day, but no buzzards had been at it yet. The brand on the shoulder was a Rocking H, the Holt brand.

Topping out on the rise, we looked into a little arroyo beside the trail. Zebony flinched, and looked around at me, his face gray and sick, and Zeb was a tough man. My horse did not want to move up beside his, but I urged it on.

The stench was frightful, and the sight we looked upon, even worse. In the bottom of that arroyo lay scattered men and horses . . . at first glimpse I couldn't tell how many.

The men were dead, stripped of clothing, and horribly mutilated. That some of the men had been alive when left by the Comanches was obvious, for there were evidences of crawling, blind crawling, like animals seeking some shelter, any shelter.

We walked our horses into the arroyo of death, and

looked around. Never had I seen such a grim and bloody sight. What had happened was plain enough. This was some of the outfit that had followed us from the Cowhouse—some of the bunch that had stolen our cattle, and from whom we had recovered the herd.

They must have circled around and gotten ahead of us and settled down here to ambush us when they were attacked. Obviously, they had been expecting nothing. They would have known they were far ahead of us, and they had built fires and settled down to prepare a meal. The ashes of the fires remained and there were a few pots scattered about. There were, as we counted, eleven dead men here.

What of the others? Had they been elsewhere? Or had some of them been made prisoners by the Indians?

Hastily, we rode up out of the arroyo, and then we got down and pulled out rocks and one way and another caved in the edge of the arroyo on the bodies to partly cover them.

"Wolves won't bother them," Zeb commented. "We haven't seen any wolves in the past couple of days."

"Nothing for them to feed on but snakes. According to Tap Henry, this country is alive with them."

We turned away from the arroyo, both of us feeling sick to the stomach. They had been our enemies, but no man wishes that kind of fate on anyone, and a Comanche with time on his hands can think of a lot of ways for a man to take time to die.

Circling the scene of the ambush, we found the trail of the departing Indians. There must have been at least forty in the band—the number could only be surmised, but it was at least that large.

Their tracks indicated they were going off toward the north, and it was unlikely they would attempt to remain in the vicinity, because of the scarcity of water. But they must have crossed this terrain many times, and might know of water of which we knew nothing. Judging from the arid lands around us, though, it was doubtful.

We had started back toward the herd when we saw those other tracks. We came upon them suddenly, the tracks of two horses.

"Well, she caught up with him," Zeb commented, indicating one set of tracks. "That's Tap's paint . . . and those other tracks belong to that little *grulla* Karen rode off. I'd know those tracks anywhere."

They had come this way . . . after the massacre in the arroyo, and they were headed due west. Before them lay the eighty miles or so to Horsehead Crossing . . . had Karen taken any water? They would need it.

We camped that night by the deep pool in the riverbed—the last water of which we knew.

CHAPTER 4

THE DEEP POOL was gone. Where the water had been was now a patch of trampled mud, slowly drying under the morning sun.

"All right, Dan," Pa said to me, "I'm no cattleman, and I have the brains to know it. You take the drive. I don't need to tell you what it means to all of us."

"There's eighty miles, or close to it, between here and Horsehead." I was speaking to them all. "But as we get close to the Pecos we may come up to some pools of water. I'll have to ride ahead, or somebody will, and spot those pools before the cattle can get wind of them, and then we'll have to keep the herd up-wind of that water.

"It's death if they drink it. Water in the pools is full of concentrated alkali, and they wouldn't have a chance.

"This is a mixed herd, the toughest kind of all to drive. From now on, anything that can't keep up will have to be left behind—any calves born on the drive must be killed.

"You know the best day we've had was about fifteen, sixteen miles. On this drive we will have to do better than that, and without water.

"The first night out, we will go into camp late and we'll start early. From that time on every man jack of you will be riding most of the day and night."

"I can ride." Conchita McCrae stood on the edge of the group. "I've worked cattle since I was a child. We want to pull our weight, and Miguel isn't up to it yet."

"We can use you," I replied, "and thanks."

Nobody said anything for a few minutes, and finally it was Tim Foley who spoke. "There's no water for eighty miles? What about the Mustang Pools?"

"We don't know, but we can't count on them. Maybe there is water there, but we will have to think like there wasn't."

Pa shrugged. "Well, we have been expecting it. Nobody can say we weren't warned. What we had best do is fill all the barrels, jars, everything that will hold water, and we had best be as sparing of it as we can."

Zebony led off, his long brown hair blowing in the wind, and after him came the brindle steer, still pointing his nose into God knows where, and then the herd.

Ben Cole and Milo Dodge rode the flanks; and behind them, Freeman Squires and Zeno Yearly.

Turning, I walked my horse back to where Tim Foley was getting ready to mount the seat of his wagon. His wife sat up there, her eyes fastened on distance.

"Everything all right, Tim?"

He turned around slowly. "No...and you know it isn't. Karen's gone, and you could have kept her, Dan."

"Me?" It was not at all what I'd expected from him. "Tim, she wouldn't have stayed for me. Nor for anyone, I guess."

"We figured you two were going to marry," Tim

said. "We counted on it. I never did like that no-account Tap Henry."

"Tap's a good man, and there was no talk of marriage between Karen and me. We talked some, but there weren't any other young folks around . . . just the two of us. And she fell hard for Tap."

"He'll ruin her. That is, if she isn't lying dead out there already."

"She's with him. We found their tracks. She caught up to him and they are riding west together."

This was no time to tell them about the massacre. I had told Pa, and some of the boys knew, because I wanted them to look sharp . . . but it might only worry the womenfolks.

If I had a wife now, well, I'd tell her such things. A man does wrong to spare womenfolks, because they can stand up to trouble as well as any man, and a man has no right to keep trouble from them, but this was Tim Foley's wife and Aaron Stark's widow, and there was Rose Sandy.

The wagons rolled, their heavy wheels rocked and rolled down into the gully and out on the other side, and we moved the cattle westward. Dust lifted from the line of their march, and the rising sun lit points of brightness on their thousands of horns. Somebody out along the line started up a song, and somebody else took it up, and glad I was to hear them, for they needed what courage they had for the long march that was ahead.

The cattle lowed and called, the dust grew thicker, and we moved on into the morning. Sweat streaked their sides, but we moved them on. Every mile was a victory, every mile a mile nearer water. But I knew there were cattle in this herd that would be dead long before we came to water, and there were horses that would die, and perhaps men, too.

The way west was hard, and it took hard men to travel that way, but it was the way they knew, the way they had chosen. Driving increases thirst, and the sun came hot into the morning sky, and grew hotter with the passing of the hours. The dust mounted.

Twice I switched horses before the morning was over. Working beside Jim Poor, I handled the drag, with Pa off in front with Zebony Lambert.

And when at last the cool of night came, we kept them moving steadily westward until at last we camped. We had made sixteen miles, a long drive. Yet I think there was a horror within us all at what lay ahead, and Conchita looked at me with wonder in her eyes. I knew what she was thinking.

We were mad . . . mad to try this thing.

We cooked a small meal and ate. We made coffee and drank, and the cattle were restless for water and did not lie down for a long time. But at last they did.

The burden was mine now. Carefully, I looked at the men, studying their faces, trying to estimate the limit of their strength.

It was late when I turned in at last, and I was the first awake, rolling my blankets and saddling the dun. Zeno Yearly was squatted by the fire when I came up to it.

He gestured at the pot. "Fresh made. He'p yourself."

Filling my cup, I squatted opposite him. "I ain't a talking man," Zeno commented, out of nowhere, "so

I've said nothing about this. Especial, as Tap is your brother."

Swallowing coffee, I looked at him, but I said nothing.

"This here range Tap located—how come that grass ain't been settled?"

"Open country. Nobody around, I reckon."

"Don't you be mistook. That there range was settled and in use before you were born."

Well, I couldn't believe it. Tap had told about that range out there, free for the taking. Yet Zeno was not a talking man, and I had never known him to say anything but what proved true.

"Tap found it for us," I protested. "He left a man to guard it."

"Tolan Banks?"

"You know him?"

"I should smile. That's a mean man, a mighty mean man. I heard Tap call his name, and I said nothing because I'm not a gunfighting man and wanted no part of Tap unless he brought it to me. That Tolan Banks is a cow-thief and an outlaw."

So there it lay. We were headed west across some godawful country, running risk of life and limb, thinking we were bound for fresh and open range, and now I found that range belonged to somebody else and we would be running into a full-scale range war when we arrived.

They say trouble doesn't come singly, and surely that was true of ours. So I drank coffee and gave thought to it, but the thinking came to nothing. For all I could see was that we were committed, and we would arrive faced with a fight—and us with starving, thirsty cattle, and folks that would be starved also.

"Zeno, you keep this under your hat. This is something I've got to study about. Seems to me, Tap should have known better."

Zeno he put down his coffee and filled his pipe. He was speaking low, for fear we would be overheard. "Meaning no offense, but it seems to me that Tap Henry is a self-thinking man. I mean, he would think of himself first. Now, suppose he wanted that land, but had no cattle? To claim land in this country you have to use it ... you have to run cows on it.

"So what better could he do, knowing you folks were discontented and talking the West? I think you will ride into a full-fledged range war, and you'll be on the side of Tolan Banks ... which puts you in a bad light."

"It isn't a good thought," I said. "I don't know this Tolan Banks."

"Like I say, he's a mean man. He will fight with any sort of weapon, any way you choose, and he's killed a lot of men. Some folks say he was one of that Bald Knob crowd, up there in Missouri. On that I couldn't say, and it seemed to me his voice sounded like Georgia to me."

We moved our herd on the trail, and they were mean. They had nothing to drink, and had not had anything the night before, nor was there water in sight.

We moved them out before the light and walked them forward, moving them steadily. And this day we worked harder than ever before. Now that water was gone, these cow-critters began thinking back to the

Cowhouse or the Middle Concho, and they had no notion of going on into this dry country. First one and then another would try to turn back.

Again, I worked the drag. Nobody was going to say that because I was in charge that I was shirking my job. At noontime we found a sort of bluff and there was shade along it for a good half-mile. We moved the herd into that shade and stopped, lying up through the hot hours.

Miguel was sitting up when I went to the wagon. "I shall be able to ride soon," he said, "and I shall help."

Glancing out, I could see nobody close by. "Miguel," I said, "we are heading for land in New Mexico."

"*Si,* this I know."

"Do you know the Mimbres Valley?"

"*Si.*" Miguel's face had grown still, and he watched me with careful attention.

"Is it claimed land?"

Miguel hesitated. "*Si*...most of it. But there is trouble there. However, the valley is long—perhaps it is not the place of which I speak."

"And Lake Valley?"

"*Si*...I know it. There is much trouble there, from the Apache...but from white men also, and from our own people, for some of them are bad, like Felipe Soto."

"Do you think we will have trouble there? We were told the range was open. It is not open, then?"

"No...and you will have much trouble." Miguel paused. "*Señor,* I regret...I wish I could ride. I know how hard it is for you."

"Have you been over this road?"

"No . . . I came from the north. I was trying to escape, and then when hurt I tried for water on the Concho."

As it grew toward evening, we started the herd once more, and Conchita was in the saddle at once, and riding her big horse. Surprisingly enough, it proved a good cutting horse, and it was needed.

Now every rider was needed. The herd slowed and tried to turn aside or turn back, but we worked, keeping them moving, pointing westward into the starlit night. At last we stopped, but the cattle would not settle down. They bawled continuously, and finally I gave up.

"Pa, let's move them. They aren't going to rest, so they might as well walk."

Once again we started, and we sagged from weariness. The men around me were bone-tired, their eyes hollow, but we pushed them on. And the white dust lifted from the parched plain, strangling, stifling, thick.

When the morning came there was no rest, no surcease. The sun rose like a ball of flame, crimson and dark, and the air was still. No slightest breeze stirred the air, which lay heavily upon us, so that our breathing required effort. And now the cattle wanted to stop, they wanted even to die, but we urged them on.

Here and there one fell out, but they had to be left. The horses slowed, and stopped, starting again with a great effort.

At the nooning the ribs of the cattle stood out, and their eyes were wild. The brindle steer stared about for something to attack, and the weary ponies had scarcely the agility to move out of the way.

We made coffee, and the riders came back to the fire one by one, almost falling from their horses, red-eyed with weariness. Yet there was no complaint. Conchita was there, her eyes great dark hollows, but she smiled at me, and shook her head when I suggested she had done enough.

Foley came to me. "Dan," he said, "we're all in. The horses, I mean. We just made it here."

"All right...let's load everything into two wagons."

Miguel hitched himself to the tailgate of the wagon. "I can ride," he said. "I prefer to ride."

Nor would he listen to anything I said, and in truth it was a help to have him on horseback, although he would be hard put to take care of himself, without trying to help us. The goods, which had thinned down owing to our eating into the supplies, were loaded into two wagons, and the team of the abandoned wagon was divided between the other two.

The bitter dust rose in clouds from the feet of the cattle, the sun was a copper flame in a brassy sky, the distance danced with heat waves and mirage. The cattle grew wearier and wearier with each succeeding mile; they lagged and had to be driven on, slapped with coiled riatas and forced back into the herd.

Here and there an aging cow fell out of the herd, collapsed, and died. Our throats burned with thirst and inhaled dust, and our shouts mingled with the anguished bawling of the thirsty cattle. And there was no respite. We pushed on and on, finding no convenient place to stop until hours past noon.

We stopped then, and a few of the cattle fell to the ground, and one horse died. The sky was a ceiling of flame, sweat streaked our bodies and made strange signs on the dusty flanks of the cattle.

As the suffering of the cattle increased, the tempers of the men shortened. Here and there I lent a hand, moving twice as much as any other hand, working desperately, the alkali dust prickling my skin, my eyes squinted against sun and trickling sweat.

It was brutal work, and yet through it all Conchita was busy. She did as much as any hand, and asked no favors. At times I even saw Miguel hazing some steer into line.

Wild-eyed steers plunged and fought, sometimes staggering and falling, but we pushed them on, and then I began moving out ahead of the herd, scouting for the poisonous water holes of which I had been warned by Tap Henry.

A thousand times I wished he had been with us, a thousand times I wished for an extra hand. For three days we did not sleep. We gulped coffee, climbed back into the saddle, rode half blind with sweat and dust, fighting the cattle into line, forcing them to move, for their only chance of survival lay in moving and getting them to water.

The brindle steer stayed in the lead. He pushed on grimly, taking on a fierce, relentless personality of his own, as though he sensed our desperation and our need for help.

And every day the sun blazed down, and long into the night we pushed them on.

Cattle dropped out, stood with widespread legs and hanging heads beside the trail. How many had we lost? How many horses worked to a frazzle?

We lost all idea of time, for the cattle were almost

impossible to handle, and we fought them desperately through the heat and the dust.

Pushing on alone, I found the Mustang Ponds, but they were merely shallow basins of cracked dry mud, rapidly turning to dust. There had been no water here in months. It was the same with the Flatrock Holes, and there was nothing else this side of the river, except far and away to the northwest what were known as the Wild Cherry Holes ... but they were off our route, and of uncertain nature.

Staring into the heat waves, it came upon me to wonder that I was here. What is it that moves a man west? I had given no thought to such a thing, although the loneliness of the far plains and the wide sky around move a man to wonder.

We had to come west or be crowded. As for the Holt crowd, we could have fought them better there than on the road. Was not this move something else? Maybe we just naturally wanted to go west, to open new country.

There have always been wandering men, but western men were all wandering men. Many a time I've seen a man pull out and leave good grass and a built house to try his luck elsewhere.

Twice I came upon alkali ponds, the water thick with the white alkali, thicker than thick soup, enough to kill any animal that drank from it.

I pushed on, and topped out on a rise and saw before me the far dark thread of growth along the Pecos. My horse stretched his neck yearningly toward the far-off stream, but I got down and rinsed my handkerchief twice in his mouth after soaking it from my canteen. Then we turned back.

We turned back, the dun and myself, and we had only some sixteen or seventeen miles to go to reach the herd.

It was a sickening sight, a dread and awful sight to see them coming. From a conical hill beside the trail I watched them.

Pa was off in front, still sitting straight in his saddle, although I knew the weariness, the exhaustion that was in him. Behind him, maybe twenty feet, and leading the herd by a good fifty yards, was that brindle steer.

And then Jim Poor and Ben Cole, pinching the lead steers together to keep them pointed down the trail.

Over all hovered a dense cloud of white dust. Alkali covered them like snow. It covered the herd, the riders, their horses . . . it covered the wagons, too.

Back along the line I could see cattle, maybe a dozen within the range of my eyes. Two were down, several were standing, one looked about to fall.

But they were coming on, and I walked the dun down the steep slope to meet them.

"Pa, we'll take the best of them and head for the river. I dislike to split the herd, but if we can get some of them to water, we can save them."

Most of them were willing to stand when we stopped, but we cut out the best of them, the ones with the most stuff left, and, with Pa leading off, four of the boys started hustling them toward Horsehead on the Pecos.

The day faded in a haze of rose and gold, great red arrows shot through the sky, piercing the clouds that dripped pinkish blood on the clouds below. The vast brown-gray emptiness of the plain took on a strange enchantment, and clouds piled in weird formations, huge towers of cumulus reaching far, far into the heavens.

Many a time I had heard talk of such things, the kinds of clouds and the winds of the world, and I knew the wonder of it. But no evening had I seen like that last evening before Horsehead, no vaster sky or wider plain, no more strange enchantment of color in the sky, and on the plains, too.

Pulling up alongside the wagons, I told Mrs. Foley, "Keep it rolling. No stops this side of Horsehead!"

She nodded grimly, and drove on, shouting at the tired horses. Frank Kelsey mopped the sweat from his face and grinned at me. "Hell, ain't it, boy? I never seen the like!"

"Keep rolling!" I said, and rode back to where Miguel was coming along, with Conchita holding him on his horse. "You, too," I said. "Pay no attention to the herd. If you can, go on to the river."

The crimson and gold faded from the sky, the blues became deeper. There was a dull purple along the far-off hills, and a faint purplish tone to the very air, it seemed. We moved the remaining cattle into the darkening day, into the slow-coming night.

Under the soft glory of the skies, they moved in a slow-plodding stream, heads down, tongues lolling and dusty. They moved like drunken things, drunken with exhaustion, dying on their feet of thirst, but moving west.

The riders sagged wearily in their saddles, their eyes red-rimmed with exhaustion, but westward we moved. The shrill yells were gone, even the bawling of the cattle had ceased, and they plodded on through the utter stillness of the evening.

A heifer dropped back, and I circled and slapped her with the coiled rope. She scarcely flinched, and only after the dun nipped at her did she move, trance-like and staggering. More cattle had fallen. Twice I stopped to pour a little from my canteen into the mouths of fallen cows...both of them got up. Some of the others would be revived by the cool night air and would come on because they knew nowhere else to go.

And then the breeze lifted, bringing with it the smell of the river.

Heads came up, they started to walk faster, then to trot, and of a sudden they burst into a head-long run, a wild stampede toward the water that lay ahead. Some fell, but they struggled up and continued on.

There was the hoofs' brief thunder, then silence, and the smell of dust.

Alone I rode the drag of a herd long gone. Alone, in the gathering night. And there was no sound then but the steady *clop-clop* of the dun's hard hoofs upon the baked ground, and the lingering smell of the dust.

The stars were out when I came up to the Pecos, and there our wagons were, and our fire.

When the dun stopped, its legs were trembling. I stepped down heavily and leaned for a moment against the horse, and then I slowly stripped the saddle and bridle from him and turned him loose to roll, which was all the care most mustangs wanted or would accept.

Zebony came in to the fire. "They've drunk, and we're holding them back from the river."

"Good...no water until daybreak." Sitting down near the fire I took the Patterson from its scabbard and began to clean it. No matter what, that Patterson had to be in shape.

"I want a four-man guard on those cattle," I said, "and one man staked out away from camp, to listen. This is an Indian crossing, too. The Comanches used it long before any white man came into this country, and they still use it."

Mrs. Stark brought me a cup of coffee. "Drink this," she said. "You've earned it."

It was coffee, all right, laced with a shot of Irish, and it set me up somewhat. So I finished cleaning my rifle, then went to the wagon and dug out my duffel bag. From it I took my two pistols. One I belted on, the other I shoved down behind my belt with the butt right behind my vest.

When I came back to the fire, Pa was there. He looked at that gun on my hip, but he said nothing at all. Tom Sandy looked around at me. "Never knew you to wear a handgun," he said, "you expecting trouble?"

"You're tired, Tom," I said, "but you get mighty little sleep tonight. I want all the barrels filled now."

"Now?" Tom stared at me. "You crazy? Everybody is dead-tired. Why, you couldn't—"

"Yes, I can. You get busy—every barrel full before we sleep."

And they filled them, too.

It was past one o'clock in the morning when I finally stretched out, slowly straightening my stiff muscles, trying to let the tenseness out of my body, but it was several minutes before I could sort of let myself go ... and then I slept.

The first thing I heard when I awoke was the water, the wonderful, wonderful sound of water. Even the Pecos, as treacherous a stream as ever was ... but it was water.

The sky was faintly gray. I had been asleep almost two hours, judging by the Big Dipper. Rolling over, I sat up and put on my hat. Everything was still.

I pulled on my boots, belted on my gun, and walked over to the fire.

What I had believed to be trees and brush along the line of the Pecos was actually the shadow cast by the high bank. The river at this point was destitute of anything like trees or shrubs. The only growth along it was a thin line of rushes. It lay at the bottom of a trough that was from six to ten feet deep. The river itself was about a hundred feet wide and no more than four feet deep at the deepest point. The plain above was of thin, sandy soil, and there was only a sparse growth of greasewood, dwarf mesquite, and occasional clumps of bear grass.

Zebony came up to the fire and sat his horse while drinking a cup of coffee. It was quiet ... mighty quiet.

The cattle, still exhausted, were bedded down and content to rest, although occasionally one of them would start for the river and had to be headed back.

"You going to lay up here?"

"No."

Tim Foley looked around at me. Tim was a good man, but sometimes he thought I was too young for my job. Me, I've never seen that years made a man smart, for simply getting older doesn't mean much unless a man learns something meanwhile.

"We're going to finish crossing, and then go upstream a few miles." I gestured around me at the row of skulls marking the crossing, and at the crossing itself. "We don't want to run into Comanches."

Zeb started to turn his horse and stopped. "Dan...!"

Something in his voice spun me around. A party of riders were coming toward us. Near as I could make out, there were six or seven.

"You wearing a gun, Tim?"

"I am."

"I'm holdin' one." That would be Zeno Yearly.

Behind me there was a stirring in the camp. I glanced across the river where the herd was lying. Four men would be over there...but what about the fifth man who was staked out? Had he seen these riders? Or had they found him first?

Conchita was suddenly close by, standing half concealed by a wagon wheel.

My eyes fastened on the man in the lead. He rode a powerful bay horse, and he was a huge man. This, I knew at once, was Felipe Soto.

He rode up to the edge of camp and I saw him look carefully around. I do not know how much he saw, for we looked like a sleeping camp, except for the three of us standing there. Foley was across the fire from them, and Zeb on his horse some twenty feet off to one side. I was in the middle, and intended it that way.

My Patterson lay on the rolled-up blankets of my bed about a dozen feet off.

"I look for Miguel Sandoval," the big man said. "Turn him over to me, and you will have no trouble."

Taking an easy step forward, I took the play away from him. "What do you mean, no trouble? Mister, if you want anybody from this outfit you've got to take them. As for trouble, we're asking for all you've got."

He looked at me with careful attention, and I knew he was trying to figure how much was loud talk and how much was real trouble.

"Look, *señor,* I think you do not understand." He gestured behind him. "I have many men . . . these are but a few. You have women here, and do not want trouble."

"You keep mentioning that," I said quietly, "but we're as ready as you are. We've had a mean drive, and we're all feeling pretty sore, so if you want to buy yourself a package of grief, you just dig in your spurs and hang on."

His men started to fan out and Zebony spoke up. "Stand! You boys stand where you are or I'll open the ball," he said coolly. "If there's to be shooting we want you all bunched up."

Soto had not taken his eyes from me, and I do not know if he had intended to kill me, but I know I was ready. Whatever notion he had, he changed his mind in a hurry, and it was Zeno Yearly who changed it for him.

"You take the big one, Dan," Zeno said conversationally. "I want the man on his right."

Soto's eyes did not leave mine, but I saw his lips tighten under the black mustache. They had not seen Zeno, and even I was not sure exactly where he was.

They could see three of us...how many more were there?

There was no use losing a good thing, so I played the hand out. "Zeno," I said, "you've gone and spoiled a good thing. Between you and the boys on the riverbank, I figured to collect some scalps."

Soto did not like it. In fact, he did not like it even a little. He did not know whether there was anybody on the riverbank or not, nor did he like what he would have to do to find out.

He knew there must be men with the cattle, and that, had they seen him coming or been warned in time, they might easily be sheltered by the high bank and waiting to cut Soto and his men to doll rags.

"I regret, *señor*"—Soto smiled stiffly—"the shortness of our visit. When we come again there will be more of us...and some friends of ours, the Comanches. You would do well to drive Miguel Sandoval from your camp."

"There was a grave back yonder," I said, "of a Mexican we found and buried."

Soto smiled again. "A good trick...only we turned back and opened the grave. There was no body."

He turned his horse and walked it slowly away from camp, but we knew he would come back, and we knew we were in trouble.

"All right," I said. "A quick breakfast and then we move out."

During the night several steers and a cow had managed to make the river, and rejoined the herd. There was no time to estimate the loss of cattle on the drive, although obviously several hundred head were gone.

We pushed on, keeping up a steady move, pausing

only at noon to water in the Pecos, whose route we were following. One or more of us trailed well behind or on the hills to right or left, scouting for the enemy.

The earth was incredibly dry and was covered over vast areas with a white, saline substance left from the alkali in the area. Wherever there had been water standing, the ground was white, as if from snow.

Pa fell back and rode beside me. "We're outnumbered, Dan," he said. "They'll come with fifty or sixty men."

We saw not a living thing. Here and there were dead cattle, dried to mere bones and hide, untorn by wolves, which showed us that not even those animals would try to exist in such a place. By nightfall there was no grass to be found, so we brought the wagons together on a low knoll, with the cattle behind it.

There was a forest of prickly pear, which cattle will eat, and which is moist enough so they need little water. Half a dozen of us went out and singed the spines from bunches of pear with torches, and it was a pretty sight to see the torches moving over the darkening plain. But the cattle fed.

With daybreak, the wind rose and the sky was filled with dust, and clouds of dust billowed along the ground, filling the air and driving against the face with stinging force. The sun became a ball of red, then was obscured, and the cattle moved out with the wind behind them, herded along the course of the Pecos, but far enough off to avoid its twistings and turnings.

By nightfall the dust storm had died down, but the air was unnaturally cold. Under the lee of a knoll the wagons drew up and a fire was built.

Zebony rode in and stepped down from his horse.

Ma Foley and Mrs. Stark were working over a meal. There was little food left, but a few of the faltering cattle had been killed, and some of the beef was prepared. The flour was almost all gone, and no molasses was left.

Zeno Yearly came up and joined us. There was a stubble of beard on his lean jaws, and his big sad eyes surveyed us with melancholy. "Reminded me of a time up on the Canadian when I was headed for Colorado. We ran into a dust storm so thick we could look up betwixt us and the sun and see the prairie dogs diggin' their holes."

Squatting by the fire, I stared into the flames, and I was doing some thinking. Pa was relying on me, with Tap gone, and I hadn't much hope of doing much. The herd was all we had, and the herd was in bad shape. We had a fight facing us whenever Felipe Soto and his Comancheros caught up with us, and we were short-handed.

We had lost several hundred head and could not afford to lose more. And from what Conchita and Miguel said, we were heading into a country where we might find more trouble than we wanted.

We were almost out of grub, and there was no use hunting. Whatever game there had been around here had drifted out, and all we could do was keep driving ahead.

Our horses had come out of it better than most, for many a herd crossing the Horsehead had wound up with most of the hands walking, their horses either dead or stolen by Indians. About all a man could do was go on; but I had found that many a problem is settled if a man just keeps a-going.

It wasn't in me to sell Felipe Soto short. He was a tough man, and he would come back. They did not want any talk of Comancheros or of the Palo Duro Canyon to get around... there already was opposition enough from the New Mexicans themselves.

"We'll push on the herd," I told Zebony. "We should reach the Delaware soon."

It was amazing how the water and the short rest had perked up the cattle. There had been little grass, but the prickly pear had done wonders for them, and they moved out willingly enough. It was as if they, too, believed the worst of the trip was past. Knowing something of the country that lay before us, I was not so sure.

We closed up the herd and kept the wagons close on the flank. Zeno Yearly and Freeman Squires fell back to bring up the rear and do the scouting. Pa led off, and part of the time was far out ahead of us, scouting for ambush or tracks. The rest of us kept the herd closed up and we moved ahead at a steady gait.

Toyah Creek, when we reached it, was only a sandy wash, so we went through and pushed on. As we traveled, we gathered the wood we found where wagons had broken down and been abandoned, for there was nothing along the trail for fuel but buffalo chips and occasional mesquite, most of which had to be dug out of the ground to find anything worth burning.

The coolness disappeared and again it became incredibly hot. The heat rising from the herd itself, close-packed as it was, was almost unbearable.

Conchita rode over to join me.

"We have talked, Miguel and I," she said. "You protected us, or we should have been killed."

"It was little enough."

"We did not expect it. Miguel . . . he did not expect to be helped, because he is a Mexican."

"Might make a difference to some folks, not to us. When we first came into this country—I mean when Pa first came—he would never have made out but for help from Mexican neighbors."

"We have talked of you, and there is a place we know—it is a very good place. There is danger from Indians, but there is danger everywhere from them."

"Where is this place?"

"We will show you. It lies upon a route used by the *padres* long ago. By traders also. But there is water, there is good grass, and I think you can settle there without trouble."

"Where will you go?"

"To my home. To Miguel's mother and his wife."

"He did not mention a wife. I thought maybe . . . Miguel and you . . ."

"No, *señor*. He is married. We are grown up in the same house, but we are friends only. He has been a very good brother to me, *señor*."

"Like Tap and me," I said. "We got along pretty good."

All through the day we rode together, talking of this thing and that. The cattle moved steadily. By nightfall we had twelve miles behind us.

There was a chance the dust storm might have wiped out miles of our tracks, and that might help a little. But in the arid lands men are tied to water, and they must go where water is, and so their trails can be found even if lost.

Ira Tilton was out on the north flank of the drive as

we neared the last stop we would make along the Pecos. From that point we would cut loose and drive across country toward Delaware Creek.

Toward sundown he shot an antelope and brought it into camp. It was mighty little meat for such a crowd of folks, but we were glad to get it.

We were of no mind to kill any of our breeding stock, which we needed to start over again, and the steers we needed to sell to the Army or somebody to get money for flour and necessaries to tide us over the first year. We were poor folks, when it came to that, with nothing but our cattle and our bodily strength for capital.

That night when the firelight danced on the weathered faces of the cowhands, we sat close around the fire and we sang the songs we knew, and told stories, and yarned. There was a weariness on us, but we were leaving the Pecos, and no cowhand ever liked the Pecos for long.

Firelight made the wagon shadows flicker. Ma Foley came and sat with us, and the firelight lit the gold of Conchita's hair to flame, to a red-gold flame that caught the light as she moved her head.

Rose Sandy came to the fire, too, sitting close to Tom, and very quiet. But I do not think there was censure among us for what she had done, for nobody knew better than we that the flesh was weak.

Pa was there, listening or talking quietly, his finecut features looking younger than he was.

"We will find a place," he said, "and we will settle. We will make of the Kaybar a brand we can be proud of."

There was hope in all of us, but fear, too. Standing

up at last, I looked at Conchita and she rose, too, and we walked back from the fire together. Miguel stood by his wagon, and when we passed him, he said, *"Vaya con Dios."*

FREEMAN SQUIRES SHOOK me out of a sleep and I sat up and groped for my hat. It was still...the stars were gone and there were clouds and a feeling of dampness in the air. Stamping into my boots, I picked up my gun and slung the belt around me, then tucked the other behind my belt.

Then I reached for the Patterson, and as I did so there was a piercing yell far out on the plains, and then a whole chorus of wild Comanche yells and the pound of hoofs.

The cattle came up with a single lunge and broke into a wild stampede. I saw Free Squires riding like mad to cut them off, saw his horse stumble and go down and the wave of charging, wild-eyed cattle charge over him.

And then I was on one knee and shooting.

A Comanche jumped his horse into camp and my first shot took him from the saddle. I saw Pa roll out of bed and fire a shotgun from a sitting position.

In an instant the night was laced with a red pattern of gunfire, streaks of flame stabbing the darkness in the roar of shooting.

Zebony Lambert ran from the shelter of a wagon, blazing away with a six-shooter. I saw an Indian try to ride him down and Zeb grabbed the Indian and swung up behind him and they went careering off into the night, fighting on the horse's back.

A big man leaped past me on a gray horse—it was the blond man who had been with Webb Holt when he was killed.

A horse struck me with his shoulder and knocked me rolling, a bullet spat dirt into my mouth as it struck in front of me.

Again I started to get up and I saw Pa firing from his knee. There was blood on his face, but he was shooting as calmly as if in a shooting gallery. Ben Cole was down, all sprawled out on the ground, and I saw Jim Poor rise suddenly from the ground and run to a new position, with bullets all around him.

Suddenly I saw Bud Caldwell charge into camp, swing broadside, and throw down on Pa. I flipped a six-shooter and shot him through the chest. The bullet hit him dead center and he was knocked back in the saddle and the horse cut into a run. Turning on my heel I fired again from the hip and Bud Caldwell fell on his face in the dirt and turned slowly over.

And as it had started, it ended, suddenly and in stillness.

The wagontop on one of the wagons was in flames, so I grabbed a bucket of water and sloshed it over the flames, and then jumped up and ripped the canvas from the frame and hurled it to the ground. A bullet clipped the wagon near me and I dropped again and lay still on the ground.

Our herd was gone. Freeman Squires was surely dead, and it looked like Ben Cole was, too.

Nothing moved. Lying still in the darkness, I fed shells into my six-shooter and tried to locate the Patterson.

Somewhere out in the darkness I heard a low moan,

and then there was silence. The smell of dust was in my nostrils, an ache in my bones; the gun butt felt good against my palm. Behind me I could hear the faint rustle of water among the thin reeds along the bank, but nothing else moved.

They were out there yet, I knew that, and to move was to die.

What had happened to Conchita? To Ma Foley? Where was Pa?

In the distance, thunder rumbled...the night was vastly empty, and vastly still. A cool wind blew a quick, sharp gust through the camp, scattering some of the fire, rolling a cup along the ground.

With infinite care, I got a hand flat on the ground and eased myself up and back, away from the firelight. After a moment of waiting I repeated the move.

Thunder rolled...there was a jagged streak of lightning, and then the rain came. It came with a rush, great sheets of rain flung hard against the dusty soil, dampening it, soaking it all in one smashing onslaught.

When the lightning flared again, I saw my father lying with his eyes wide to the sky, and then the lightning was gone, and there was only the rumble of thunder and the rush of rain falling.

CHAPTER 5

IN A STUMBLING run I left the place where I lay and ran to my father's side.

He was dead. He had been shot twice through the body and had bled terribly.

Taking the rifle that lay beside him, I leaped up and ran to the nearest wagon and took shelter beneath it. If any of the others lived, I did not know, but my father was dead, our cattle gone, our hopes destroyed, and within me, suddenly and for the first time, I knew hatred.

Under the wagon, in partial shelter, I tried to think ahead. What would Soto and his men do? All my instincts told me to get away, as far away as possible before the morning came, for unless I was much mistaken, they would come to loot the wagons.

How many others were dead? And did any lie out there now, too grievously wounded to escape? If so, I must find them. Knowing the Comanche, I could leave no man who had worked with us to fall helpless into their hands.

Carefully, I wiped my guns dry. The Patterson still lay out there somewhere, but I had my father's breech-loading Sharps. The shotgun he had also had must still be lying out there.

The storm did not abate. The rain poured down

and the Pecos was rising. It was a cloudburst, or something close to it, and the more I considered it the more I began to believe that my enemies might have fled for shelter, if they knew of any. Or perhaps they had gone off after our cattle, for without doubt they would take the herd.

Suddenly, in the wagon above me, there was a faint stir of movement. Then thunder rumbled in the distance, and lightning flashed, and on the edge of the riverbank, not twenty yards off, stood two bedraggled figures. I knew them at once.

Tim Foley and his wife!

They lived, at least. And who was in the wagon? One of us, I was sure ... yet could I be sure? Perhaps it was some Comanche who had started to loot the wagon.

Carefully, I eased out from under the wagon. The rain struck me like a blow, the force of the driven rain lashing viciously at my face. It would be completely dark within the wagon, and I would be framed against the lightning, but I must know. The Foleys were coming, and they must not walk into a trap.

One foot I put on a horizontal spoke of the wheel, and, holding to the edge of the wagon with my left hand, I swung myself suddenly up and into the wagon.

There was a startled gasp.

"Conchita?"

"*Dan!* Oh, Dan! You're *alive*!"

"More or less. Are you all right?"

"Of course, but this man is hurt. He has been shot."

Risking a shot myself, I struck a light. It was Zeno Yearly, and there was a graze along his skull and a

crease along the top of his shoulder. Evidently the bullet had struck him when he was lying down in the
wagon, and grazing the side of his skull, it had burned
his shoulder. He had bled freely, but nothing more.

The rain continued without letup, and through the
roar of the rain on the canvas wagon cover we heard
the splash of footsteps, and then Ma Foley and Tim
climbed into the wagon.

Zeno sat up, holding his head and staring around
him.

"It's safe, I think, to light a candle," I said. "They
have gone or they would have shot when I struck the
match."

When a candle was lighted I rummaged in the
wagon for ammunition.

"Here," Tim Foley said, holding out the Patterson,
"I found it back there."

Taking the gun, I passed the Sharps over to him,
and began cleaning the Patterson, wiping the rain and
mud from it, and removing the charges.

"Are we all that's left?" Ma Foley asked plaintively.
"Are they all gone?"

"Pa's dead, and I saw Squires go down ahead of the
stampede. I saw Ben Cole fall."

"Jim Poor got down under the bank. I think he was
unhurt then, if the river didn't get him."

Huddled together, we waited for the morning, and
the rain continued to fall. At least, there would be water. We must find and kill a steer, if we could find a
stray. And somehow we must get to the Rio Grande,
or to the Copper Mines.

For we had been left without food. What had not
been destroyed in the brief fire in the other wagon was

undoubtedly damaged by the rain, although I hoped the damage would be slight. And there had been little enough, in any event.

Our remuda was gone, the horses stolen or scattered, and the chances of catching any of them was slight indeed. The trek that now lay before us would in many ways be one of the worst that anyone could imagine, and we had women along.

The responsibility was mine. These were our people, men who worked for us, and my father was dead. In such a case, even with the herd gone, I could not, dared not surrender leadership. Now, more than ever, we needed a strong hand to guide us out of this desert and to some place where we might get food and horses to ride.

Fear sat deep within me, for I had encountered nothing like this before, and I feared failure, and failure now meant death...at least, for the weakest among us.

All the night long, the rain fell. The Pecos was running bank-full, and so would be the arroyos leading to it. Our way west was barred now by one more obstacle, but, once the sun came out, the arroyos would not run for long, and their sandy basins, long dry, would drink up the water left behind. Only in the *tinajas*, the natural rock cisterns, would there be water.

The sun rose behind a blanket of lowering gray cloud, and the rain settled down to a steady downpour, with little lightning, and thunder whimpering among the canyons of the far-off Guadalupes.

Stiffly, I got to my feet and slid to the ground. Donning my slicker, I looked carefully around.

The earth was dark with rain, the ground where the

camp stood was churned into mud, and wherever I looked the sky was heavy with rain clouds that lay low above the gray hills. The Pecos rushed by—dark, swirling waters that seemed to have lost their reddish tinge. Crossing the camp, I picked up Pa's body and carried it to shelter under the wagon, then began to look around.

On the edge of camp I found Bud Caldwell...he was dead. Another man, unknown to me, but obviously a Comanchero, lay dead near the riverbank.

Ignoring their bodies, I gathered the body of Ben Cole in my arms and carried him to where Pa lay.

We desperately needed horses, but there were none in sight. There was a dead horse and a saddle lying not too far away and, walking to them, I took the saddle from the horse, tugging the girth from beneath it. The horse lay upon soft mud, and the girth came out without too much trouble. Then I removed the bridle and carried them to the wagon.

Tim Foley got down from the wagon. "Tim," I said, "you and Mrs. Foley can help. Go through both wagons and sort out all the food you can find that's still good. Also, collect all the canteens, bedding, and whatever there is in the way of ammunition and weapons."

He nodded, looking around grimly. "They ruined us, Dan. They ruined us."

"Don't you believe it. We're going to make it through to the Copper Mines, and then we'll see. If you find Pa's papers, account books and the like, you put them aside for me."

Zeno Yearly got down from the wagon also. He looked wan and sick, but he glanced at me with a droll smile. "We got us a long walk, Dan. You much on walking?"

Together we hunted around. There was no sign of Jim Poor, but he might have been drowned or swept away by the river.

The one thing none of us was talking about was the kids. Tim's two boys and Stark's children. Nobody had seen a sign of them since the attack, yet I had seen them bedded down and asleep when I was awakened to go out for my night guard.

Zeno and me walked slowly up along the bank of the river. Whatever tracks there had been were washed out. It was unbelievable that they could all have survived, but the fact that we saw no bodies gave us hope.

Zeno and I spread out, and suddenly he gave a call. He was standing looking down at or into something. When I got over there, I saw that he was standing on the edge of some limestone sinks.

The earth had caved in or sunk in several places that were thirty feet or more in diameter. Looking across the hole where Zeno stood, we could see the dark opening of a cave.

Zeno called out and, surprisingly, there was an answering call. Out of a cave under the very edge where we stood came Milo Dodge.

"Heard you talkin'," he said. "You all right?"

"You seen the youngsters?"

"They're here with me, all dry and safe. Emma Stark is here, too."

Slowly, they climbed out of the cave and showed themselves. Milo climbed up to where we were.

"Frank Kelsey's dead. He lived through the night,

died about daybreak. He caught two damned bad ones, low down and mean . . . right through the belly."

"Pa's dead," I said, "and Ben Cole."

"Emma Stark got the youngsters out when the first attack hit, and I'd seen this place, so I hustled them over here. I got in a couple of good shots, and missed one that I wished had hit."

"What do you mean?" He had a look in his eyes that puzzled me.

"Ira Tilton," Dodge said. "He was with them. When they came riding in he was alongside Bud Caldwell. I took a shot at him."

"Remember the fight Tap had with Webb Holt? If Ira was with them, that explains how those other men showed up so unexpectedly. He must have warned them."

"I'll make it my business," Milo said coldly. "I want that man."

"You'll have to get to him before I do," Zeno said. "I never liked him."

Slowly we gathered together, and it was a pitiful bunch we made.

Tim Foley, Milo Dodge, Zeno Yearly, and me . . . three women, five children. Foley's boys were fourteen and ten . . . Emma Stark's youngsters were a girl thirteen, and two boys, one nine, one a baby.

"First off," I said, "we'd better move into that cave, Milo. The women and youngsters can hide there while we hunt horses. I can't believe they were all driven off, and I think we should have a look around. Some of those horses may come back to camp."

We stripped the wagons of what was left that we could use, and took only the simplest of gear. We moved our beds and cooking utensils down there, and what little food was left, and we moved our ammunition, too.

Zeno and I started out in one direction, each of us with a rope. Milo and Tim started out the other way. Unluckily the storm had left no tracks, but we had agreed not to go far, to keep a wary eye out for Comanches, and if we found nothing within a few miles, to return.

Zeno and me climbed a long, muddy slope to the top of the rounded-off ridge. The country was scattered with soapweed, prickly pear, and mesquite. Far off, we saw something that might be a horse, or maybe a steer—at that distance, we couldn't make it out.

"There's another!" Zeno picked it out with his finger. "Let's go!"

We started off, walking in the direction of the animal we had seen, and when we had gone scarcely half a mile we could make it out to be a steer. It was Old Brindle, our lead steer.

"You ever ride a steer, Dan?"

"When I was a youngster—sure. I don't think anybody could ride Old Brindle, though."

"Maybe," Zeno looked at him with speculative eyes. "Toward the end there, he was getting mighty friendly. Acted as though he and us were handling that herd together. Let's go get him."

Well, we walked along toward him, and pretty soon he sighted us. We saw his big head come up—his horns were eight feet from tip to tip—and then he walked out toward us, dipping his horns a little as if ready for battle. A man on the ground is usually fair game for any steer, although they will rarely attack a man on horseback.

He came toward us and I spoke to him, and he watched us, his eyes big and round, his head up. Turning away, I started toward that other animal. "Come on, boy!" I said. "You're with us."

And you know something? That big old steer fell in behind us like a big dog, and he walked right along, stopping when we stopped, moving when we moved.

"He might stand for a pack," I said, "and if he did, it would take a load off us."

"We can try."

And then we had a real break.

Rounding the clump of mesquite that lay between us and the other animal we had seen, we saw it. Standing there in a sort of hollow was that lineback dun of mine, and with him were two other horses from the remuda. One was a bay pony, the other a paint.

I called out to the dun, and he shied off, but I shook out a loop. He ducked and trotted around, but when the loop dropped over his head he stood still, and I think he was glad to be caught. Horses and dogs thrive better in the vicinity of men, and they know it. Moreover, they are sociable animals, and like nothing better than to be around men and to be talked to.

Rigging a hackamore from some piggin strings, I mounted up, and soon had caught the paint. Zeno was packing the bridle I'd found on Bud Caldwell's dead horse—if it was his—and he was soon riding the second horse. The third one was more shy, but he seemed to want to stay with the other horses, and when we started back toward camp he followed along and pretty soon Zeno dabbed a loop on him.

Foley and Dodge returned empty-handed. They had seen fresh tracks, however, made since the rain, of both cattle and horses.

We camped that night in the cave, and made a sparing supper of the remnants of some salt pork and beans.

"This cave goes away back," Foley commented. "Looks like the whole country's undermined with it. I used to live in a limestone country in Kentucky, and believe me, caves like this can run for miles."

At daybreak we loaded what gear we had and moved out. The youngsters and the women were to take turns riding, and surprisingly enough, Old Brindle seemed pleased with his pack. That cantankerous old mossyhorn was full of surprises, but he had gotten used to folks, and he liked being around them. Not that Conchita and the youngsters hadn't helped by feeding him chunks of biscuit or corn pone touched with molasses.

We made a sorry outfit, but we started off. The bodies of Pa and the others were buried in a row, and what little we could find of Freeman Squires.

There was no sign of Zebony Lambert, of Jim Poor or the Sandys.

The last I'd seen of Zeb he had jumped on a horse behind a Comanche and gone riding away into the night, fighting with him. Maybe he was a prisoner, and maybe he got off scot-free. Anyway, we had found no other bodies, though in hunting horses we had looked around a good bit.

We kept going, and by nightfall came up to a place in the bend of Delaware Creek. There had been a big encampment here at some time in the past, and there was a lot of wood lying about, and one busted-down wagon from which two wheels had been taken.

The grass was the best we had seen in weeks, and there were a couple of clumps of mesquite of fair size.

About sundown Zeno killed an antelope, and we had antelope steaks for supper. It was the first good meal we had since leaving the Pecos.

We took turns standing guard, for we figured we weren't finished with the Comancheros, and wanted to be ready for them. It was nigh on to midnight when I heard a horse coming. He was coming right along, but when he got somewhere out there in the darkness, he stopped.

My dun whinnied, and he answered, and came closer. It was Conchita's big horse.

Shaking her awake, I explained, and she got up quickly and went to the edge of the firelight, calling him. He came right up to her and started to nuzzle her hand as if looking for corn or sugar or something. He was wearing a saddle and bridle of Spanish style, with a high cantle and too much tree for my taste. There was a good rifle in the scabbard, and the saddlebags were evidently packed full.

Conchita opened the saddlebags. There were a couple of small packets of ammunition and a buckskin sack containing some gold pieces.

She handed this to me. "We can use that," she said.

Nothing had been said about Miguel, but I could see by the stillness of her face and a tightness around her eyes that she was trying to maintain her composure. His body had not been found, and nobody could recall seeing him after the first burst of fighting.

Obviously, the big horse had been captured along with the rest of the stock, but he had thrown his rider at some later time and returned to us.

"No man had ridden him," Conchita explained. "He would have watched for his chance to throw any rider but myself, or perhaps some other woman."

We moved westward, and the clouds withdrew and the sun came out. Heat returned to the plains ... the grass grew sparser again, there was little fuel. We men walked ... and we saw no Indians.

On the third day we killed an ox we found on the desert. Obviously left behind by some wagon train passing through, perhaps long before, he had fattened on mesquite beans. We killed and butchered the ox, and that night we dined on good beef and cut much of the remainder into strips to smoke over the fire.

In the distance we could see the tower of Guadalupe Mountain shouldering against the sky.

Surprisingly, we made better time than with the herd and wagons. On the first day after finding Conchita's horse we put sixteen miles behind us, but we made dry camp that night.

Morning came and we were moving out before dawn, with Zeno and myself off in the lead. The women and youngsters on the horses came in between, and Tim Foley brought up the rear with Milo Dodge.

The desert shimmered with heat waves, and on the open plain weird dust devils danced. A chaparral cock appeared from out of nowhere and ran along beside us. Everywhere we passed what had been pools from the rain, now dried up, the earth cracked and turning to dust. Our canteens were nearly empty, and there was no food left but the strips of dried, smoked beef.

The soil was hard and gravelly; there were frequent limestone outcroppings, and low hills. Westward was the beckoning finger of Guadalupe Mountain. Toward dusk we made camp in a little valley where the grazing was good. There were a few trees here, and three springs, one of them smelling strongly of sulphur and a soda spring, but the third was pure, cold water.

Foley helped his wife from the saddle, and for a moment they stood together, her arms clinging to his. Her naturally florid features were burned even redder by the sun and wind, but she was pale beneath the color, and he led her carefully to a place under a tree, where she sat down.

The children scattered to gather wood and cow chips for a fire, and Zeno led the horses into the shelter of the trees.

Tim Foley walked over to where I stood talking to Zeno Yearly. "My old woman's about had it, Dan. She's done up. If she don't get some food and proper rest soon, we won't have her with us long."

"You're looking kind of long in the tooth yourself, Tim," I said, "but you're right. Seems like we'd better get some meat before we pull out of here."

"This is Apache country," Milo Dodge said, "so keep an eye out."

It was finally settled that I would go alone, and the other three would remain behind to keep a sharp lookout. Foley's boy was provided with a rifle, for he was fourteen and coming on to manhood, and they settled down to guard the womenfolks and the horses.

Wearing my two pistols, with the Patterson fully loaded, I walked out. Twice I saw rattlers, but I left them alone.

The evening was still. The desert was gathering shadows in the low places, and the distant mountains were taking on the soft mauve and purple of evening. Somewhere out on the desert a quail called ... and after a minute, there was an answer. These were the blue quail, which rarely fly, but run swiftly along the ground. They were small, scarcely larger than a pigeon.

Twice I paused, and with piggin strings, the short strips of rawhide carried by a cowhand for tying the legs of a calf, I rigged several snares where I had seen rabbit tracks.

But I found no game. Toward dusk I did get a shot at a quail, and killed it. Returning home, I had only the quail to show. At daybreak I checked my traps and found I'd caught a large jackass rabbit. What meat there was on him was divided among the women and children.

So we started on at the break of dawn. The Guadalupe Peak loomed higher than ever, and the long range that stretched out to the north from behind it seemed dark and ominous. Tim Foley, who was the oldest of us all, fell down twice that day. Each time he got up slowly, carefully, and came on.

We camped that night after making only a few miles, in a small grove of live oak and pines, with the mountain looming over us.

Tim Foley dropped to the ground, exhausted, and it was Milo and Zeno who stripped the saddles from the horses and helped the women down. Taking my Patterson, I walked out at once.

To tell you the truth, I was scared. We men had gone a whole day without food, and during the past four or five days had been on mighty short rations. Tim was older than we were, and had lived a life in the saddle, but it was still a good long trek to the Copper Mines for all of us.

Nobody had much to keep them going, and if I did not scare up food of some kind we were not going much farther.

Several times I saw deer droppings, but all were old, and I saw no deer, nor any recent tracks. Because this was Apache country, I did not wish to shoot unless I was sure of a kill.

It was very still. Sweat trickled down my chest under my shirt. The sky overhead was very blue, and the clouds had gone. For some reason my nerves were suddenly on edge, yet I had heard nothing, seen nothing. Carefully, I edged forward.

Far overhead a lone buzzard circled lazily against the blue. The vague trail I followed now had carried me over a thousand feet above the tiny valley where our camp lay concealed. Drying my hands on my shirt, I started forward again. Suddenly, on the edge of a cliff some fifty yards away, I saw a bighorn sheep.

He was a big fellow, and he was watching something below him. His big horns curved around and forward, and he had the color of a deer, or close to it, and the same sort of hair. It was the first bighorn I had seen.

Carefully, leaning my shoulder against the cliff, I lifted the Patterson and took a careful sight on a point just back of his neck. I was trying for a spine shot, hoping to stop him where he was. Shot through the heart, he might disappear into the rocks and be lost. Deer will often run half a mile after a heart shot and the bighorn might do even more, and this was a rugged country.

But even as I laid the sights on the point where I wished the bullet to strike, the poise and attention of the sheep worried me. Lowering the rifle, I eased forward a step farther, and looked down into the rugged country below.

The first thing I saw was a cow...it was a white-faced longhorn cow, and then behind it came another and another, and they were our cows. And then a man stepped from the brush. It was Jim Poor!

Holding still, I watched them slowly come from a draw onto the open mountainside, at least thirty head of cattle, some cows, some young stuff, and a few old steers, and behind them walked two men, and a woman who rode their one horse.

Catching myself just as I started to call out, I looked again at the bighorn. He had drawn back and turned away from me, and he was ready to get out of there, and fast. Lifting the Patterson, I caught my sight again, and squeezed off the shot.

The bighorn leaped straight up and landed with his legs spread out. He started to go forward and I steadied the rifle for another shot. Just as I was about to fire, his knees buckled and he fell forward on one shoulder and lay still.

Glancing into the basin below, I saw no one. Only the cattle, standing now with their heads up, staring, nostrils distended. Grinning, I lowered my rifle and, knowing how a voice can carry in that still air, I called out.

"You boys scared of something? A body'd think you all stepped on a hot rock!"

"Dan? Dan Killoe?" That was Zeb's voice.

"If it ain't," I yelled back, "then Pa fed me for a long time for nothing!"

They came out in the open then, and I saw that the woman on the horse was Rose Sandy, and the men were Zeb Lambert, Jim Poor, and Miguel. And then another came from the brush, and it was Tom Sandy!

I let out a whoop and started to go down the mountain, then remembered that sheep.

"Jim! Come on up here! I've killed me a bighorn!"

He clambered up the slope. "You're a better butcher than I am, Jim, so skin him out and I'll talk to those boys and then come on up and help you pack it in."

The horse on which Rose was riding was the one Zebony had taken from that Indian he rode off behind. He had been well outside the circle of the fighting before his battle with the Comanche ended, and by the time he started back the rain was pouring down and the fighting was about over.

The country was covered with Comanches and Comancheros, so he had found a place where a notch cut into the riverbank and concealed himself there with the horse. He had put in a wet and miserable night, but at daybreak he saw some cattle to the south and started around to gather them, and then he met Rose and Tom Sandy.

Miguel was with them, and in bad shape. He had been captured by the Indians, had killed his captors and escaped, but had been wounded again. These, though, were merely flesh wounds, and he had recovered quickly in the succeeding days.

Banding together, they had rounded up what strays they could find and started off to the northwest, heading toward a limestone sink Miguel knew of. There they had found water and some friendly Lipans, who traded some corn and seeds they had gathered for a steer.

Twenty miles west they had come upon Jim Poor. He was standing beside a horse with a broken leg... he had ducked to the shelter of the riverbank, but caught a horse whose owner had been shot, and when the shooting died down, believing everyone in the camp was dead, he had started west alone.

———

NINE DAYS LATER we reached El Paso, a small town of one-story adobe houses, most of it lying on the Mexican side of the river. On the north side of the river there were several groups of settlements, the largest being Coon's Rancho and Magoffinsville, the two being about a mile and a half apart. There was a third settlement, about a mile from Magoffinsville, around another ranch.

Zebony came to me after we had found shelter and had our small herd, once more led by Old Brindle, gathered in a pasture near the town.

"Dan, what are we going to do?"

"What we started to do," I said. "At least, I am. I'm going on, and I'm going to find us an outfit, and I'm going to use what cattle we have to start a ranch."

"And then?"

"Why, then I'm going hunting. I'm going hunting for a man with a spider scar, a man named Felipe Soto."

Pausing for a second, I considered the situation. Around me I had a lot of good folks, and they had come west trusting to work for my father and myself, and it was up to me to see they made out. Yet there was scarcely more than fifty dollars among the lot of us, and cattle that we dearly needed. And to go on, we must have horses, gear, and supplies of all kinds.

Ahead of us lay miles of Apache country, and where we would settle would probably be Apache country, too. Being a slow man to anger, the rage against Soto and his Comancheros had been building up in me, and I feared it.

There was in me a quality I had never trusted. A quiet sort of man, and scarcely twenty-three, I liked to work hard and enjoyed the pleasure of company, yet deep within me there was a kind of fury that scared me. Often I'd had to fight it down, and I did not want the name of being a dangerous man—that is for very young boys to want, or older men who have never grown up. Yet it was in me, though few of those about me knew it.

Pa knew—he had been with me that time in San Antonio; and Zebony knew, for he had been with me in Laredo.

And now I could feel it mounting. Pa was dead, cut down in the prime of life, and there were the others, good men all. They were men who rode for the brand, who gave their lives because of their loyalty and sense of rightness.

Within me I could feel the dull fury growing, something I had felt before. It would mount and mount until I no longer thought clearly, but thought only of what must be done. When those furies were on me there was no fear in me, nor was there reason, or anything but the driving urge to seek out my enemies.

My senses became super-sharp, my heart seemed to slow its beat, my breath seemed slower, I walked with careful step and looked with different eyes. At such times I would become utterly ruthless, completely relentless. And I did not like it.

It was the main reason that I rarely wore a handgun. Several times the only thing that had saved me was the fact that I carried no gun and could not do what I wished. Twice in my life I had felt these terrible furies come over me, and each time it left me shaken, and swearing it must not happen again.

Now there were other things to consider. We must find horses, a wagon, and the necessary supplies for the rest of our trip. Our herd was pitifully small, but it could grow. We had two young bulls and about twenty head of cows, mostly young stuff. The rest were steers, and a source of immediate profit, even if their present value might be small.

Some of the people at Magoffinsville preferred to call their town Franklin. Others were already calling the town on the American side El Paso del Norte, but most still referred to the three towns by their separate names. At Magoffinsville I tied the lineback dun at the rail in front of James Wiley Magoffin's place and went in. Zebony Lambert and Zeno Yearly were with me.

Magoffin was a Kentuckian who had come to the

area thirteen or fourteen years earlier and had built a home. Then he erected stores and warehouses around a square and went into business.

When I walked through that door, I knew there was little that was respectable in my appearance. My razor had been among the things lost in the attack, and I had not shaved in days. My hat was a beat-up black, flat-crowned, flat-brimmed item with a bullet hole through the crown. I wore a worn, fringed buckskin shirt and shotgun chaps, also fringed. My boots were Spanish style, but worn and down at heel. The two men with me looked little better.

"Mr. Magoffin," I said, "the Comancheros took my herd. We're the Kaybar brand, moving west from the Cowhouse to new range northwest of here, and we're broke. We came into town with only our women and children riding, and the rest of us afoot."

He looked at me thoughtfully. "What do you want?"

"A dozen horses, one wagon, supplies for seventeen people for two weeks."

His eyes were steady on me, then he glanced at Zebony and Zeno Yearly.

"Women, you say?"

"Yes, sir. The wives of two of my men, the widow of one, and there's five children, and a single girl. She's from New Mexico."

"Mind if I ask her name?"

"Conchita McCrae."

He glanced over my shoulder toward the door, and I felt the hackles rise slowly on the back of my neck. Turning slowly, I saw Felipe Soto standing there, three of his men behind him.

My fist balled and I swung.

He had expected anything but that. Words...perhaps followed by gunplay, but the Texan or New Mexican rarely resorted to his fists. It was not, in those days, considered a gentleman's way of settling disputes, while a gun was.

My blow caught him flush on the jaw. Being six feet two inches tall, I was only a little shorter than he was, but half my life I'd been working swinging an axe, or wrestling steers or broncs, and I was work-hardened and tough. He did not stagger, he simply dropped.

Before the others could move, Zebony covered them with a pistol and backed them up.

Reaching down, I grabbed Soto by the shirtfront and lifted him bodily to his feet, slamming him back against the counter. He struck at me, and I slipped inside of the blow and smashed a wicked blow to his belly and then swung to his chin.

He fought back, wildly, desperately, and he was a huge man and strong, but there was no give in me that day, only a cold burning fury that made me ignore his blows. He knocked me down...twice, I think. Getting up, I spread my legs wide and began to swing, and I was catching him often. I drove him back, knocked him through the doors into the street, and went after him. He got up and I smashed a wild swing to his face, then stabbed a wicked left to the mouth and swung on his chin with both fists.

He was hitting me, but I felt none of it. All I wanted was to hit him again. A blow smashed his nose, another split a lip through to the teeth. Blood was pouring from a cut eye, but I could not stop. Backing him against the hitch rail I swung on his face, chopping it to a bloody mess.

And no one stopped me. Zeno had a six-shooter out now, too, and they kept them off.

Soto went down and tried to stay down, but I would not let him. I propped him up and hammered on him with both fists until his face was just raw meat. He fell down, and grabbed at the muddy earth as if to cling to it with all his might.

He was thoroughly beaten, and Magoffin stepped forward and caught my arm. "Enough!" he said. "You'll kill the man!"

My hands were swollen and bloody. Staggering, I stepped back, shaking Magoffin's hand from my shoulder.

Soto lay in the mud, his huge body shaking with retching sobs.

"Tell him," I said to the Soto men, "that if I see him again—anywhere at all—I'll kill him.

"And tell him, too," I added, "that I want my herd, three thousand head of cattle, most of it breeding stock, delivered to me at Bosque Redondo within thirty days.

"That will include sixty head of saddle stock, also driven off. They will be delivered to me or I shall hunt him down and beat him to death!"

With that, I turned and staggered against the door post, then walked back into the store. Magoffin, after a glance at Soto, followed me inside. Zebony and Zeno stood watching the Soto men pick up their battered leader and half drag, half carry him away.

"That was Felipe Soto?" Magoffin asked me curiously. "I have heard of him."

"That was him," I replied. My breath was still coming in gasps and my heart was pounding. "I should have killed him."

"What you did was worse. You destroyed him." He hesitated. "Now tell me again. What was it you needed?"

"You must remember," I said, "I have only fifty dollars in money."

"Keep it—your credit is good with me. You have something else—you have what is needed to make good in this country."

Conchita turned pale when she saw me, and well she might, for in the excitement of the fight I had scarcely felt the blows I received, and they had been a good many. One eye was swollen almost shut, and there was a deep cut on the other cheekbone. My lip was puffed up, one ear was swollen, and my hands had swollen to twice their normal size from the fearful pounding I had given him.

"Oh, your poor face!" she gasped. Then at once she was all efficiency. "You come here. I'll fix that, and your hands, too!"

She poured hot water into a basin with some salts, and while she bathed my face ever so gently, my swollen hands soaked in the hot water.

It seemed strange, having a woman fuss over me that way, and it was the first time it had happened since one time as a youngster when Tap's mother had taken care of me after I'd been bucked from a bad horse.

That started me thinking of Tap, and wondering what had become of him, and of Karen.

The Foleys never talked of her around the camp,

and what they said among themselves I had no idea. She had taken on more than she was equipped to handle when she followed after Tap, and it worried me.

Everybody was feeling better around camp because Zebony and Zeno had told them about the deal I had made with Magoffin. Not that it was so unusual in those times, for a man's word was his bond, and no amount of signatures on paper would mean a thing if his word was not good. Thousands of head of cattle were bought or sold on a man's word, often with no count made when the money was paid over. Because of that, a man would stand for no nonsense where his word was concerned. A man might be a thief, a card cheat, and a murderer, and still live in the West; but if his word was no good or he was a coward, he could neither live there or do business with anyone there.

"You reckon that Soto will return your cattle?" Tim Foley asked skeptically.

"If he doesn't, I'll go get them. I have told him where he stands, and I shall not fail to carry out my promise."

"What if he takes to that canyon?"

"Then I shall follow him there."

We had a camp outside of Magoffinsville. It was a pretty place, with arching trees over the camp and a stream running near, and the Rio Grande not far off. It was a beautiful valley with mountains to the north and west, and there seemed to be grapes growing everywhere, the first I'd ever seen cultivated.

We sat around the fire until late, singing the old songs and talking, spinning yarns we had heard, and planning for the future. And Conchita sat close beside me, and I began to feel as I never had before. It was a different feeling because for the first time I knew I wanted a girl ... wanted her for always, and I had no words to speak what I thought.

Soon we would be on the trail again, moving north and west into the new lands. Somewhere up there was Tap Henry, and I would be seeing him again ... what would be our relationship, now that Pa was dead?

Tap had respected Pa ... I did not think he had such respect for me. He was too accustomed to thinking of me as a youngster, yet whatever we planned, Tap could have a share in it if he would do his part to make our plans work out.

I got up and walked out to where the horses were, and stood there alone in the night, looking at the stars and thinking.

Magoffin would supply us with what we needed, but the debt was mine to pay. We had few cattle to start with, and such a small herd would make a living for nobody. Whatever happened, I had to have the herd they had stolen, or the same number of cattle from elsewhere.

If Felipe Soto did not bring the cattle to me, I was going after them, even to Palo Duro Canyon itself.

Conchita came up to where I stood. "Are you worried, Dan?"

"They came with me," I gestured back toward the people at the fire; "they trusted my father and me. I must not fail them."

"You won't."

"It will be hard."

"I know it will, Dan, but if you will let me, I want to help."

CHAPTER 6

WE CAME UP the valley of the Mimbres River in the summer of fifty-eight, a handful of men with a handful of cattle and one wagon loaded down with supplies.

We put Cooke's Spring behind us and trailed up the Mimbres with the Black Range to the east, and on the west the wilderness of the Mogollons. We rode with our rifles across our saddlebows, riding through the heart of Apache country, and we came at last to our Promised Land.

The Plains of St. Augustine, a vast inland sea of grass, surrounded by mountains, made the finest range we had ever seen, with nothing in sight but a few scattered herds of antelope or wild horses.

Our camp was made in the lee of a cliff close by a spring, with a bat cave in the rocks above us. We turned our cattle upon the long grass, and set to work to build a pole corral to hold our saddle stock.

Cutting poles in the mountains, we came upon both bear sign and deer sign. Zeno Yearly stopped in his cutting of poles. "It is a fair land, Dan, but I've heard tell this is an Indian trail, so we'd best get set for trouble."

"We're building a fort when we have the corral, but first we must protect our saddle stock."

The fort was not so much to look at, not at first. We made a V of our wagons, pointing it toward the open valley, and we made a pile of the poles for the corral along one side, and threw up a mound of earth on the other side, with the cliff behind us. Though it was not much of a fort, it was a position that could be defended.

Three days later we had our Texas house built, with the Foleys occupying one side and the Stark family the other. We had also put up most of a bunkhouse, and had our cattle fattening on the long grass. We had scouted the country around, killed a couple of deer and a mountain lion we caught stalking a heifer from our herd.

We were settling in, making a home of the place, but it was time I made a move.

News was beginning to filter through to us. There was trouble down in the Mimbres Valley—a shooting or two, and the name we heard was that of Tolan Banks, the man Tap Henry had mentioned.

And then one day they came riding up the valley, Banks and Tap, and a third man with them. It was the blond man who had ridden with Caldwell.

Tap was riding a grudge, I could see that. He rode up and looked around. "What the hell is the idea? I thought you were going to settle down in the Mimbres with us?"

"Before we talk about anything else," I said, "you tell that man"—I indicated the blond man—"to start riding out of here. If he comes around again, I'll kill him."

"He's a friend of mine," Tap replied. "Forget him."

"Like hell I will. He was one of those who ran off our cattle. He was in the attack on us when Pa was killed."

Tap's face tightened. "I heard about that. I couldn't believe it."

Zebony was standing by the corral, and Milo Dodge was in the door of the Texas with Jim Poor.

"You tell that man to leave, Tap."

His face stiffened. "By God, kid, you don't tell me what to do. I'll—"

My eyes held them all, but mostly the blond man. "You," I said, "start riding. And keep riding. When I see you again, I start shooting."

The man touched his tonguè to his lips. "You think you—"

I shot him out of his saddle.

A moment there had been silence, and then I was holding a gun with a slow twist of smoke rising from the muzzle, and the blond man was on the ground.

Whatever Tolan Banks might have done he did not do, for Zebony was holding a rifle in his hands, and so was Milo.

"Tap," I said, "you pick that man up and ride out of here. You're welcome any time, but when you come, don't come with a murdering renegade like him."

My bullet had gone a little high, and the man was shot through the shoulder, but from the look of it, he was badly hurt.

Tap Henry sat very still on his horse, and there was a strange look in his eyes. It was as if he was seeing me for the first time.

"I'll come back, Dan. I'll come back looking for you. Nobody talks to me like this."

"You're my brother, Tap, by raising if not by blood. I want no trouble with you, but when you start traipsing around with men who have attacked us, it is time to ask where your loyalty lies."

"You'll be seeing me, too," Banks said.

My eyes swung to him. "I was wondering when you were going to put your ante into this game," I said, "and I'm ready any time you are."

He sat his horse, smiling at me. "Not now...not right now. You've too many guns against me."

"Ride out of here then."

Banks turned his horse and Tap got down to help the wounded man into the saddle. Jim Poor came down to help him.

"You come back when you want, Tap. But come alone or with Karen, and come friendly."

"Where is Karen?" Tim Foley demanded.

"She's in Socorro," Tap said sullenly. "She's all right."

Foley held a shotgun. "Are you two married?"

Tap glanced at him bleakly. "You're damned right," he said. "What do you think I am?"

"Take care of her," Foley said. "I'm no gunfighter, but this shotgun doesn't care who it shoots."

Tap rode away, leading the renegade, who was swearing in a high, plaintive voice.

There I stood, in the sun of a bright day, watching them ride off down the valley. There went Tap, who had been my hero as a youngster, and there went the last of whatever family I had, and I watched him go and was lonely.

Ours was a hard land, and it took hard men to ride it and live it, and the rules had to be laid down so all could read, and the lines drawn.

Tap Henry was different. It seemed to me Tap was

rootless, and being rootless he had never quite decided where he stood, on the side of the angels or against them. Well, today should force him to a decision. He knew where I stood.

If that blond man had been trying to sneak a gun on me, I was not sure . . . nor did I much care. He had been there when my father was killed, and was as guilty as if he himself had fired the shot—and he might have.

One thing I had learned. It saves a lot of argument and trouble, and perhaps mistakes leading to greater violence, if folks know exactly where you stand. We came to a raw and lonely land, a land without law, without courts, and with no help in time of danger. There were men who wished the land to remain lawless, for there were always those who were unable to abide by the rules of society; and there were others who wanted schools, churches, and market days, who wanted homes, warm and friendly. Now I had taken my stand . . . I had drawn a line that no man could mistake.

After they had gone, nobody had any comment to make. The work picked up where it had ceased, and went on as it always must; for birth, death, and the day-to-day matters of living never cease. There are meals to be prepared, cattle to be cared for, meat to be butchered, fences to be built, wood to be cut. For while man cannot live by bread alone, he must have the bread before other things can become real. Civilization is born of leisure, and leisure can come only after the crop has been harvested.

In our hearts we knew that, for lonely men are considering men, given to thought to fill the empty hours of the lives they live.

Yet now the time had come to ride eastward, to be

sure that we recovered our herd. I doubted if it had yet been sold, and while my warning to Soto might cause him to deliver the herd, I doubted that it would. Even if he wanted it so—which I doubted—there were others involved.

"Tim," I said, "I'm riding after the herd. I'm leaving you in charge. Jim Poor and Tom Sandy will stay with you—and Miguel."

"I go with you, Dan." Miguel looked up from the *riata* he had been mending. "It is better so. Soto, he has many friends, and we are a people who protect our own. If you go among them, a stranger, all will be against you, even if they lift no hand.

"If I go with you to tell what Soto has done, and that you are good people, your enemies will be only the Comancheros." He smiled. "And I think they are enough for trouble."

There was no arguing with him, for I knew what he said to be the truth. The Spanish-Americans of Texas and New Mexico were clannish, as they had a right to be, and I would be a stranger among them, and a *gringo*. They would know nothing of the facts of my case— whether I was a true man or false. In such a case they would either ignore me or actively work against me.

And then Conchita declared herself. She, too, was coming. She had much to do. She must go to Socorro. There were things to buy . . . In the end, she won the argument, and she came with us.

Zebony, Zeno Yearly, Milo Dodge, Miguel, and myself made up the group. It was a small enough party for what we had to do.

Socorro was a sleepy village on the Rio Grande, built on the site of a pueblo. A mission had been established there as early as 1628, but during the Pueblo revolt the people had fled south and established a village of the same name on the Rio Grande, returning in 1817 to reestablish the village. All this Conchita told me as we rode toward the village from the west.

Though we were a small number, we were veterans at the sort of trouble that lay before us. Growing up on the frontier in Texas is never easy, and Zebony had killed his first Kiowa when he was thirteen. He had spent a week dodging Comanches even before that, and had seen his family killed.

Zeno Yearly had come west from Kentucky and Tennessee, where he had lived at various places along the Natchez Trace and in the mountains. Most of his life he had lived by hunting. Milo Dodge had been a Texas Ranger with Walker, and had served as a boy in the army during the War with Mexico.

We rode into Socorro, a tight, tough little band. And there we would buy supplies and start east, for we had far to go to reach the land of the Comanchero.

It was cool in the little *cantina* where we went to drink and to listen. Conchita was in the store, and her brother had disappeared somewhere among the flat-roofed adobe houses.

We four went into the *cantina* and ordered the wine of the country, for they were raising grapes and making wine at Socorro, as at El Paso and elsewhere. There were old apple trees here, too, planted long ago by the friars, or so it was said.

Zebony put his hat on the table and combed out his long brown hair, hair fine as a woman's and as beautiful. Yearly watched him, touching his long mustache from time to time.

There was a stillness within us, a waiting. Each knew what lay beyond this place. For out there was a wild and lonely land where the Apaches roamed, and beyond that, where we were going, the Comanche—great horsemen and great fighters, and we were few, going into a harsh land where many enemies awaited us. But this was what we had to do, and not one of us would draw back.

The wine was good, and after a while the owner brought us each a huge bowl of *frijoles,* a stack of *tortillas,* and some eggs scrambled with peppers and onions.

Miguel came in, standing inside the door until his eyes became accustomed to the dimmer light, and then he crossed to our table and sat down. Leaning toward us, his eyes very bright, he said, "It is well that we came here, for my friends tell me something very interesting."

We looked at him, and waited. Miguel took out his *cigarito* and put it between his lips.

"Soto is not at Palo Duro...he is on the Tularosa."

"That's east of here, ain't it?" Zeno asked.

"It is a place—a very small place which I think will get no larger because of the Apache—a place called Las Placitas. It is near Fort Stanton, where there are soldiers."

He lighted his *cigarito.* "It is tell to me that Soto brings his cattle there to sell to the soldiers."

"I didn't know there was a fort over there," Dodge said. "Stanton, you say? There was a Captain Stanton killed there a few years back."

"*Si,* it is name for him. The fort was built...1855, I think. So these people come to the Rio Bonito and they begin a settlement, but I think the Apache will run them out."

"Soto is there?"

"*Si*...with many men. And a large herd of cattle and some horses."

"Why, then," I said, looking around the table, "that is where we will go."

We walked out on the boardwalk and stood there together, four men looking up and down the street, and knowing that trouble might come to us at any time.

And then I saw Karen.

Or rather, Milo Dodge saw her. "Dan...look."

She was coming toward us, and I thought she looked older, older by years, and she looked thinner, too. As always, she was, neat, and when she saw us she almost stopped; then, chin up, she came on.

"Karen...Mrs. Henry," I said, "it is good to see you again."

"How do you do?" We might have been strangers. She spoke and started to pass on. "Your folks are still with us. Tap knows where we are, and they would like to see you."

She had gone past us a step when she stopped and turned slowly around. "I do not think you like my husband," she said.

"Whenever you folks feel like coming home," I said, "there's a place for you. Pa left no will, and though he sent Tap away, that makes no difference. If Tap wants to come back, it will be share and share alike."

"Thank you."

She started away, then stopped again. Maybe it was something in our manner, maybe it was just the way we were armed, for each one of us was carrying a rifle, and each had two or more pistols.

"Where . . . what are you doing?"

"We're going after our cattle, Karen," I said. "Felipe Soto has them over at Las Placitas."

"But . . . there's so many of them! You won't have a chance! Why, there must be twenty men with him—or even twice that many."

"Yes, ma'am, we know that, but they're our cattle."

That was how we felt about it. They were our cattle, so we must go after them, and thieves must not be permitted to escape the consequences of their deeds. We had a land to build, we had peace to bring to the land, and for a few years now we would have to bring it with a gun. To the violent, violence is the only argument they understand. Justice they understand, but only when it is administered from strength.

Before the sun was over the eastern mountains we were miles upon our way. We crossed some desert, we crossed the lava flows, and we came up through the live oak and the pines to the mountains and the Rio Bonito. We followed it along toward the cluster of adobes and shacks along the stream.

There were scarcely half a dozen, and a few tents, a few tipis. We spread out as we came into the town, and beyond the town we could see the herd. There were some men on horseback where the cattle were, and some of them wore plumed helmets and blue uniforms. That would be the cavalry.

We rode our horses down there, and we saw men come into the street behind us and look after us. A couple of them started to follow.

"One thing," I said, "this here's my fight. If anybody

comes in that ain't asked, you boys do what you've a mind to...but I will do the talking and if it is man to man, I'll do the shooting."

They understood that, but I wanted it on the line so they could read the brand of my action.

Felipe Soto was there, and when I saw who was with him I felt something turn cold inside of me. Tolan Banks was there, and Tap Henry.

There were eight or nine of them, and four or five Army men inspecting that beef.

Walking my horse up to them, I saw Banks speak suddenly, and Soto turned sharply around.

I did not take my eyes from Banks and Soto. "Captain," I said, "these are stolen cattle, stolen from me. The brands have been altered, but skin any beef here and you will find a K Bar brand before it was changed."

"I am buying beef," the Captain replied coolly, "not fighting over it, or sitting as a court in judgment of ownership." He turned his horse. "When you have decided whose beef it is, I shall be in Las Placitas."

He turned his horse and, followed by his brother officers and a couple of sergeants, he started away.

My eyes sought them out, man by man. On each man I directed my attention, and on each I let my eyes rest for a minute. I wanted each man to believe that he was marked.

"Well, Soto, you did not deliver the beef. I have come for it."

"Dan—!" It was Tap. "Dan, for God's sake!"

"Tap," I said, "you'd better decide where you stand before the shooting starts. Riding the fence can give a man a mighty sore crotch, and you've been on it long enough."

"Now, wait!"

"To hell with that, Henry!" Tolan Banks yelled suddenly. "You're with us or against us! Stand aside and let me kill that Killoe whelp!"

What I did, they did not expect. For years Tap and me had practiced shooting on the run, shooting while riding at a dead run, like the mountain men did, and I slapped spurs to that lineback dun and he jumped right into the middle of them.

They outnumbered us, so as I jumped into them I jumped shooting.

It looked like a damned fool trick, but it was not. They had been sitting there as we came up and no doubt every one of them had picked a target. They had us cold and we had them the same way, and in about a split second a lot of men were going to die.

Starting off with a cold hand that way, a man can shoot accurately, and I would be losing men. So I jumped my horse into their group, which forced them all to move, and each had to swing to get on his target again.

My Patterson was across my saddle, and as I jumped I shot. My bullet missed Soto and knocked a man behind him sidewise in the saddle, and then I was in among them. One more shot left the Patterson before it was knocked from my grip, but I had already come out with a draw with my left hand from my belt.

Soto swung on me and his gun blasted almost in my face. Knocking his gun up, I shot and saw him jump back in the saddle like he'd been struck with a whip. He shot at me again but I had gone past him and he turned fast, but his big horse was no match for that dun, who could turn on a quarter and give you twenty cents change. The dun wheeled and we both shot and my bullet hit him right below the nose.

He swung around and fell back out of the saddle, kicking his foot loose from the stirrup at the last minute. He started up, gun in hand, blood flowing from his face in a stream. But I went in on a dead run, holding my six-shooter low and blasting it into him. I saw the dust jump from his shirt twice as I went into him, and then he went down under the dun's hoofs and I wheeled around in time to see Tap Henry facing Tolan Banks.

"I'm with them, Tolan! That's my brother!"

"To hell with you!" Banks's pistol swung down in a dead aim on Tap's chest and Tap triggered his gun charging, as I had.

Banks left his saddle and hit the ground and rolled over, all flattened out. He made one heave as if he was trying to get up, and then he lay still.

The gray dust lifted and slowly swirled and settled, and the riderless horses trotted off and stood with their stirrups dangling and their heads up, and men lay on the ground.

Yearly was down, and Zeb was gripping a bloody arm, his face gray.

Four of them were down, and I knew my jump into them had given us the break we needed, for my boys had been sitting still taking dead aim.

The Army came riding up. One of the men rode right to Zebony. "Here! Let me see that arm! I'm a surgeon!"

We rode around, looking at the men on the ground. Felipe Soto was dead, and of the others only one man was alive.

Among the dead was Ira Tilton. I had never even seen him in the brief encounter, nor did I know whose bullet had put him down, but he had died an ugly death.

By the look of it the slug had been one of large caliber and it must have hit the pommel of the saddle or something, because the wound looked like a ricochet. It had ripped across the belly, and he had died hard, a death I would wish for no man.

I turned to the officer as he rode up. "Captain, that man was Felipe Soto." I indicated the sprawled body of the big Comanchero. "He has been selling rifles to the Indians for years. His own people will tell you of it."

"I am buying cattle," the Captain replied, "and personal feuds are not a part of my business. However, I do know of Soto, but did not realize that was who it was."

He glanced at me. "My name is Hyde. It is a pleasure to know you, sir. That was a nice bit of action."

Zebony picked up my Patterson from the ground and handed it to me. "You'd better see the Doc. You're bleeding."

"I'm all right. I just—" Glancing down, I saw there was blood on the skirt of my saddle, and my left leg was sopping with it.

"You!" the surgeon said. "Get down here!"

It was Tap who caught me when I started to get down and almost fell. He steadied me with an arm to a place under a tree, and he pulled my shirt off.

A bullet had gone through my side right above my hipbone, but the doctor merely glanced at it. "You've lost a lot of blood, but it's only a flesh wound."

Hearing a pound of hoofs, I looked around in time to see Conchita throw herself from her horse and come to me. The doctor looked at her, then at me. "If she can't make you well," he said dryly, "nothing can."

Zeno was going to be all right. He had caught two slugs, and he was in bad shape, but he was going to pull through. Tap Henry told me that some time later, for about the time that Conchita arrived everything faded out. I had started to speak, and then everything blurred. The next thing I knew it was hours later and I was in bed at the Fort.

"Are the cattle all right?"

"Sold 'em," Tap said, "all but a couple of hundred head of breeding stock."

"Looks like I'll be here for a while," I said, "so you'd better take the boys and start for home with that herd."

"Dan." Tap hesitated, as embarrassed as I'd ever seen him. "I've been a fool. I'm...well, I never intended for the herd to go to Bosque Redondo. Banks and me wanted to use it to grab land on the Mimbres."

"I guessed it was something like that."

He looked at me for several minutes. "Dan, I'm going to let Karen ride back with the boys. I'll wait here until you can ride, and we'll go home together."

"Sure," I said, "that's the way Pa always wanted it."

About Louis L'Amour

*"I think of myself in the oral tradition—
as a troubadour, a village tale-teller, the man
in the shadows of the campfire. That's the way
I'd like to be remembered—as a storyteller.
A good storyteller."*

IT IS DOUBTFUL that any author could be as at
home in the world re-created in his novels as
Louis Dearborn L'Amour. Not only could he physi-
cally fill the boots of the rugged characters he wrote
about, but he literally "walked the land my characters walk." His personal experiences as well as his
lifelong devotion to historical research combined to
give Mr. L'Amour the unique knowledge and understanding of people, events, and the challenge of the
American frontier that became the hallmarks of his
popularity.

Of French-Irish descent, Mr. L'Amour could trace
his own family in North America back to the early
1600s and follow their steady progression westward,
"always on the frontier." As a boy growing up in
Jamestown, North Dakota, he absorbed all he could
about his family's frontier heritage, including the story
of his great-grandfather who was scalped by Sioux
warriors.

Spurred by an eager curiosity and a desire to
broaden his horizons, Mr. L'Amour left home at the

age of fifteen and enjoyed a wide variety of jobs, including seaman, lumberjack, elephant handler, skinner of dead cattle, miner, and officer in the transportation corps during World War II. During his "yondering" days he also circled the world on a freighter, sailed a dhow on the Red Sea, was shipwrecked in the West Indies and stranded in the Mojave Desert. He won fifty-one of fifty-nine fights as a professional boxer and worked as a journalist and lecturer. He was a voracious reader and collector of rare books. His personal library contained 17,000 volumes.

Mr. L'Amour "wanted to write almost from the time I could talk." After developing a widespread following for his many frontier and adventure stories written for fiction magazines, Mr. L'Amour published his first full-length novel, *Hondo,* in the United States in 1953. Every one of his more than 120 books is in print; there are more than 300 million copies of his books in print worldwide, making him one of the bestselling authors in modern literary history. His books have been translated into twenty languages, and more than forty-five of his novels and stories have been made into feature films and television movies.

His hardcover bestsellers include *The Lonesome Gods, The Walking Drum* (his twelfth-century historical novel), *Jubal Sackett, Last of the Breed,* and *The Haunted Mesa.* His memoir, *Education of a Wandering Man,* was a leading bestseller in 1989. Audio dramatizations and adaptations of many L'Amour stories are available from Random House Audio publishing.

The recipient of many great honors and awards, in 1983 Mr. L'Amour became the first novelist ever to be awarded the Congressional Gold Medal by the United

States Congress in honor of his life's work. In 1984 he was also awarded the Medal of Freedom by President Reagan.

Louis L'Amour died on June 10, 1988. His wife, Kathy, and their two children, Beau and Angelique, carry the L'Amour publishing tradition forward with new books written by the author during his lifetime to be published by Bantam.

FORGET THE LAW OF THE JUNGLE...

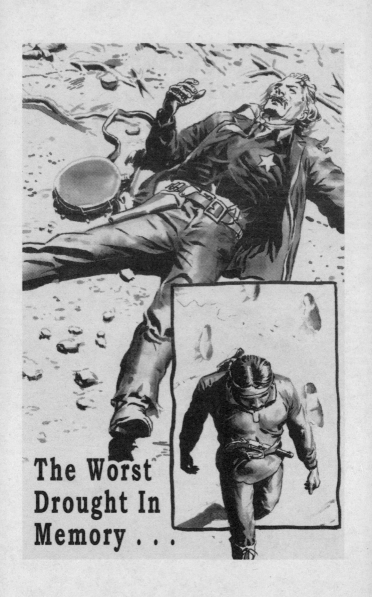

The Worst
Drought In
Memory . . .

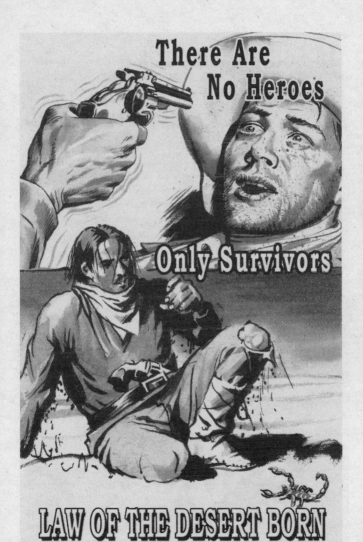

Praise for
Law of the Desert Born

"This actually may be the story's ideal form....
The result is stunning and richly textured."
—*Publishers Weekly*

"Yeates' artwork is incredible."
—GraphicNovelReporter.com

"*Law of the Desert Born* is a fantastic
example of how relevant the Western can be."
—Suvudu.com

"The richer plot and characters from
L'Amour's son Beau and collaborator Kathy
Nolan add appeal and value in addition to
the finely crafted visuals."
—*Library Journal*

"The novel's illustrations add a new
dimension to an already gripping tale."
—*American Cowboy*

"An amazing level of detail and ambience
that breathes new life into Louis L'Amour's
already stunning story."
—*Cowboys & Indians*

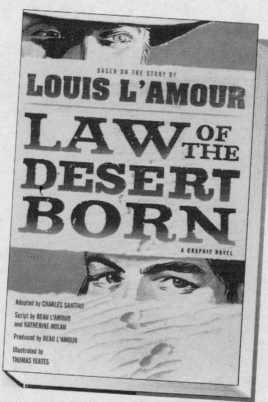